Building the Dream

Andrea Warrilow

The second book in the series

At the Cliff Top

Building the Dream

ISBN: 9798673619360

Independently Published

Printed by Amazon

.First Edition.

Acknowledgements

With huge thanks to my husband Paul, who has worked tirelessly, helping me edit this book.

Thanks again to Carola Rush for the lovely cover.

Thanks also to Leanne Regan for reading the draft and giving feedback.

Glossary of Terms

I have used some horse terminology that you may not be familiar with. I hope these definitions help

Lunge/lunging – Exercising a horse by using a long rope attached to it's head wear and having the horse go round you in big circles, usually without a rider on board.

Hack/Hacking – to ride your horse out in the country-side or on the roads.

Head Collar – simple head wear for horses used for leading them around or tying them up. Not used for riding generally.

Bridle – Leather head wear for horses, used when riding to help control the horse.

Saddle – Leather seat strapped onto horses back for riding on.

Stirrups – Metal pedals, hanging from saddle, for riders' feet to go in.

Strangles – Very infectious disease in horses, usually not fatal but spreads very easily and makes them quite ill.

Rain Scald – Sore and scabby skin condition that can affect horses who spend long periods standing in the rain. Usually on their backs.

Buck/Bucking – Like a rodeo horse, arched back, legs and body thrown upwards into the air, Horses do this for a few reasons such as pain, excitement, naughtiness or fear. It is a behaviour that often unseats a rider.

Cob – Stocky horse with strong legs.

Mare – female horse.

Gelding – castrated male horse.

Chestnut – horse colour – brown all over, often a gingery brown.

Piebald – Horse colour. Usually mainly white with irregular black splodges, like Friesian cows.

Feathers – the long hairs on some horses' legs, near their hooves. Common in cobs.

Hay – long grass, dried, cut and baled to feed livestock in winter, or when unable to graze on fresh grass.

Straw – The stalks of wheat or other corn, dried, baled and used as bedding for horses and other livestock.

Key to Plan

1. Cottage Garden

2. Farmhouse

3. Courtyard

4. Stables / Hayloft above

5. Outdoor Arena

6. Muck Heap (old silage pits)

7. Hay / Straw Barn

8. Cattle Barn

9. Machinery Barn

10. Vet Centre

11. Quarantine Centre

Close up of Farm Buildings

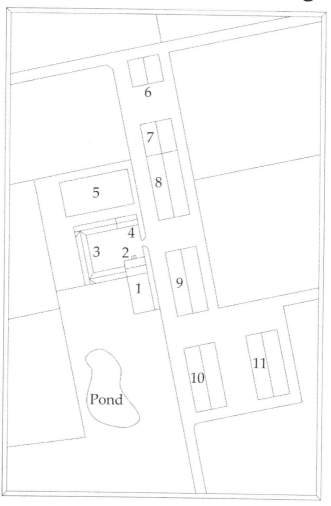

Plan of Cliff Top Farm

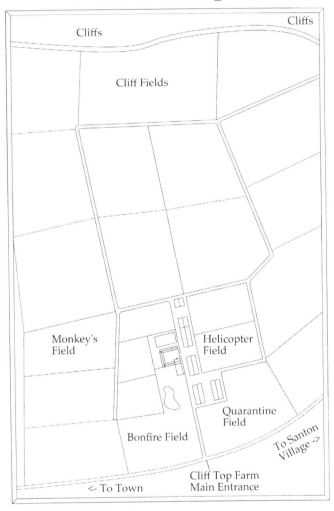

Chapter 1

Waiting

Carrie was sitting on an old kitchen chair, in the courtyard, enjoying some late sunshine. Pickle, a cat they had taken on with the farm, sat beside her sharing the warm afternoon. Although it was nearly October, there was still a little heat in the sun. She had spent a very dirty, dusty day cleaning out the old stables and was taking a quick break. They had discovered the four stables, some months ago, on the ground floor of the two-storey building, opposite their new back door. Of old-fashioned construction, the stables had quality. They had wooden partition walls, the top halves of which were more open, constructed with metal bars. They had a lovely warm and cosy feel, with old ceramic mangers for feed and heavy metal wall racks for hay. The four stables were served by a fairly wide central aisle, so the mangers and hay racks could be filled from outside the stables themselves. The old stable doors were made of solid wood, with years of wear and patina that was beautiful. Because of the way the stables were constructed each one had at least one outside, stone wall. In each stone wall was a large, opening window which made the stables seem light and would keep them cool in summer. Carrie could imagine horses' heads looking out of the windows and enjoying the view of the fields or the yard. The floors were made of concrete but she imagined that was a later addition – at least it would be easy to sweep out.

She hoped to move her horse, Bilbo, to the farm soon and she wanted these stables clean and cosy for him. There was a big hayloft above the four stables which she had to clean first – the floor was made of old wooden floorboards up there and she didn't want the years of old hayseeds and dust falling through into the stables after she cleaned them. It had been an exhausting day but she was nearly done. The hard work had kept her mind occupied so she didn't get too excited about tomorrow's monumental event. Her wonderful fiancé Caleb was coming home! He had been away filming in the US for nearly 3 months and she missed him like crazy. The last six or eight months had all been pretty crazy, to be honest. She thought back over that time, reliving the huge and dramatic changes in her life, and smiled to herself.

It had all started with a chance meeting, in a restaurant, where she hadn't even realised who Caleb was, despite his huge fame. Caleb Kirkmichael was one of the most well-known actors in the US and across the world. Carrie had been more interested in the guy dining with him, who happened to be an old friend from college. They all ended up sharing a table, so Carrie could reminisce with her college friend. According to Caleb, that was when he fell in love with her. Over the next few months, they had hardly seen each other at all. She was still wrapped in the grief of losing her first husband and Caleb was waiting and hoping she would one day heal enough to love again. Eventually, they got to spend a few days together, while Caleb was looking at farms for sale in the south of England. Cliff Top farm was the one he chose and that's where she was now.

Around that time, she finally realised her grief was part of her history, she shouldn't be letting it spoil her present. Caleb revealed his feelings for her and she realised she felt the same. They got engaged that very day. It was also the day that Caleb's offer for the farm was accepted. Their purchase of the farm had completed a couple of weeks ago and Carrie had been living there and cleaning up since then. Caleb had been away since July, he had missed the

3

completion day for the farm purchase, having to sign the paperwork and courier it across from the US. She had visited him in the US once since he left. They had a wonderful few days getting to know each other more and meeting his parents. Now Caleb would be home tomorrow and their future could begin for real.

She sighed and got to her feet. "If you read about the last year of my life in a novel, you wouldn't believe the story at all!" she said out loud. The cat, her only company at the moment, didn't answer and, frankly, seemed pretty disinterested. She gave him a stroke and got up. "Just the last stable to disinfect then I'm done for today. Then I must ring Sally and check Bilbo's OK. I miss my horse, my 'other man', nearly as much as I miss Caleb," she told the cat, smiling. Sally was her old boss and the owner of the stable yard where her horse was staying until she could get the farm ready. It was because of Sally they had been in the restaurant all those months ago and met Caleb. She was Carrie's close friend, and agony aunt during her grief, as well as her boss. They'd known each other since soon after Carrie's first husband's death. Leaving Sally, and the lads she shared her old house with, was probably the only downside of her wonderful new life. She hoped they would visit soon for a catch-up, she really missed them all, and she wanted to show them the farm.

In the last couple of weeks, since the farm had been theirs, she had been very busy. She had got quotes for basic repairs to the courtyard outbuildings. They wanted to protect them and stop them deteriorating until they decided what they were doing with each part. She had thousands of bales of hay stored in one of the big barns and a good stock of straw bought in too. The previous owner of the farm had retired, so Caleb negotiated to buy all his hay, farm implements, tools and two tractors, ready for when they needed them. The retiring farmer had also employed a man to help him with the day to day work on the farm. With Caleb's agreement, she had offered the man a similar job working for them, and they were waiting for his decision. Apparently, his wife had insisted they have a holiday before he decided. Carrie suspected the poor woman had waited a few years for that holiday and wasn't letting the chance slip away. They should be back any day now.

Carrie knew that Caleb wanted to make some big changes inside the house, so she couldn't do much work in there. They'd talked of fitting a new 'green' heating system, improving the insulation and designing better bathrooms as well as curing a few damp patches. With that in mind, she knew she couldn't do much decorating. She had, however, bought some cheap emulsion and painted the walls of their new bedroom. She'd chosen a lovely bed for them and found some useful bits of furniture that would do for now. Luckily the delivery guys had been happy to carry the bed upstairs and assemble it for her. All the other bits she moved were small enough for her to lug around alone. Years of mucking out stables and riding horses had given her good muscles. The farmer had left quite a bit of furniture, as agreed during the sale, so she only had to move things around a bit. There was already a wardrobe built into one corner of the bedroom so she gave that a coat of paint. It was not pretty or antique and she suspected it would be taken out eventually. She'd chosen a muted lilac and white colour scheme for the bedroom and hoped Caleb would like it. It was hard to choose things with him so far away. She wished she had known him longer and knew his tastes better. She spent ages cleaning the rooms they would use straight away, it seemed silly to do much cleaning and decorating anywhere else. The three other bedrooms and the dining room could remain untouched. The sitting room had an old sofa, which she had covered with a throw, and a couple of

Victorian looking cupboards. After a good clean she decided it would do for now. She had a TV to bring from her old home, but there was no satellite TV connection, so there was no rush for that. She had a feeling, having been apart for months, they would find other things to fill their evenings for a while!

The kitchen was already fairly clean and cosy, so she just gave everything a good wash down and stocked the cupboards. She had a fridge freezer delivered and there was an Aga to cook on, the rest could wait. She had brought some cutlery, crockery, towels and bedding from her old house, but not much else. Her house-mates were still living in the house and she didn't want to leave them short. The bathrooms were OK for now and she had done a deep clean in those.

One of the first jobs they had done, even before the sale was completed, was to have a high-speed broadband connection put in. It would be needed long term for Caleb's film work, but the short term priority was so they could Skype each evening while Caleb was away. He told her he needed to see her smile every day.

Outside, the courtyard she had been working in

was a three-sided yard, with the back of the house and an open shed down one side. Some sheds and animal pens formed the back and a variety of pens plus the two-storey stable building formed the third side. All the buildings were made of the same stone as the house and were so lovely, if not a bit run down. It was wonderful to step out of the back door and feel protected and surrounded by these buildings.

In the long run, the farm with its 140 acres of grazing land and two huge steel barns, would be turned into Cliff Top Animal Shelter and Re-homing Facility. They had decided, though, that the court-yard would probably be just for their own animals and any poorly animals needing round the clock care. They wanted to keep it as their private space most of the time. They were not planning to open to the public, as such, but they did plan on having a few staff, so it would be nice to keep this area private.

Caleb's successful career as an actor meant that he had the funds to fix up the place, and he had been planning it for years in his head. It was his dream life, which had kept him going in recent years, when the novelty of Hollywood society had worn off and he craved a 'real' existence. Despite being an animal lover, he hadn't even had his own pets for years as his work took him all over the world. His plan was to surround himself with animals now. He would still act, if the right films were offered, acting was his great love, but he was giving up the rest of his time and energy to his dream. He was not even sure if acting jobs would be offered to him if he hid himself away in the English countryside, but it was a risk he was ready to take.

They were planning to rescue and re-home horses mainly, with other pets being included as time went on. The ultimate goal was to have an on-site vet and an expert team to deal with the whole process. As Caleb had said before, all he could bring was the money and a hands-on approach. But his money could employ people with the skills and experience to make it work.

Carrie had come from a recent life of existing on minimum wage and she was still struggling to get her head around Caleb's wealth. It had never occurred to her one person could earn so much over one, fairly short, career. The excesses of the film industry were beyond her comprehension. His wealth had certainly not been his attraction for her. She felt really guilty about letting him buy her extravagant things. She still couldn't get out of the habit of 'making do', it seemed wrong to overspend or waste stuff. Luckily, although his past had been full of excesses, Caleb was now wanting to use his wealth for something good. He sensed the need to be environmentally aware and was learning about modern 'green' technology with enthusiasm, to see which bits he could install for the farm. Carrie and Caleb shared a love of old buildings and wanted a home with character and heart. This was the reason he had invited her to help him hunt for a property, or at least one of the reasons! Carrie and Caleb had both fallen in love with this farm, even before they had admitted their love for each other, they were a good match.

By 3pm Carrie had finished the stables and had one last job to do outside. She really wanted Bilbo at the farm as soon as possible, so she needed to choose a field to put him in. She knew he was prone to being overweight and, even this late in the year, the grass could hold lots of goodness. Ideally, she wanted him near the house, but the obvious field, at the front, had very good lush grass in it, which would be too much for Bilbo's diet. She walked around all the nearest fields, checking the grass and also checking fences and water troughs. There was one small field at the back of the courtyard that was perfect. It looked like the grass had been grazed by the last owner's cattle quite recently, the stalks were short and all the lush grass was gone. What was left should be fibrous and lower in goodness. Perfect for a boy who had to watch his weight. She had a quick search to make sure the field was safe and the gate shut securely, then she headed back to the house. Another few jobs to tick off her list. She would find herself some dinner, have a final check the house was ready for Caleb and then sit and read while she waited for his evening Skype call.

Caleb's call connected at 8pm. "Hi Beautiful, how's your day been?" he asked as soon as he saw her on the screen.

"Very dirty," she replied grinning.

"Not necessarily what a man wants to hear from his fiancé when he's thousands of miles away!" He laughed.

She told him a few of the jobs she had done that day and explained why she had been so dusty and dirty. She had found out early on, it was better not to admit to all the jobs she did each day, as Caleb

11

started to worry she was doing too much. She didn't think he realised how much physical work she was used to doing at Sally's stable yard, and how fit she was. Better he sees the results of all her work when he got home than have him worry about her while he was away.

"Are you all packed and ready to come home?" she asked. "I can't wait for you to get here."

"Umm, about that......the filming has overrun today and they are begging us to stay another day so we can re-shoot one last scene. I told them I couldn't stay long but I think I might have to stay at least one more day. I'm really sorry sweetie but I don't feel I can refuse, even though I want to."

Carrie felt devastated, but she understood that he had no choice. She was quiet for a second, to get her emotions under control, then she said, "Of course you should stay, I am happy enough pottering here. Is it likely to run over another day, or can I get excited about you arriving on Friday?"

"I really hope we can nail it tomorrow. Hopefully, I can rearrange my flight for Friday morning and be home Friday night. I'll tell them that is all I can do, to make sure they pull all the stops out and get it finished. I am sorry my love, I know you're on your own and I really miss you."

"We've waited this long, another day will just make us even happier to be together. I'm sad you have to stay longer but I'm fine. Although, I don't even have my 'other man' here for company, just the cat, and he's not very talkative!"

"Oh, don't say that, I feel bad enough as it is. You have the car, why don't you drive up to see Bilbo and Sally?"

"I keep thinking about it, but then I feel so peaceful and close to you, in spirit, here. I don't want to leave. I'm loving making it a comfy home for us, even though most of what I'm doing is a temporary fix. At least I can make it liveable until we can make long-term decisions. I think I'll go shopping for a few bits tomorrow and maybe make arrangements for Sally to bring Bilbo here next week. I have a stable and field ready for him and she said she would bring him, in her lorry, as soon as I was ready. She'll love to see you again and see the farm. You can tell her how well Simon did with his riding on set, she'll be proud we helped him get his confidence back."

Carrie and Sally had helped another actor to overcome his fear of riding so he could ride a horse in the film.

"Simon was ace, you'd never have guessed he'd been so nervous. It would be lovely to get Bilbo settled at the farm, will he be OK on his own though? I know horses are happiest in a herd."

"I think he will, but we need to get him some company soon, I don't like to think of him alone for long. I'll see if Sally knows of any horses needing a retirement home or something."

"Good idea, we can take on our first needy case if you can find one! I'll know, by tomorrow night when I can get home, so at least we can plan. I hope I'll see you Friday. Good night my sweetie, I love you so much."

"I love you too Caleb, see you very soon, sweet dreams."

She switched off the computer and let out a sigh of frustration and disappointment. "Never mind, it's only another day, I'll live," she said out loud, to convince herself.

She decided to phone Sally while she was thinking
about it. Sally reported that Bilbo was well and
happy. She hoped she and Terry could bring him to
the farm next Wednesday and spend an afternoon
with them. Sally's new assistant, Carrie's
replacement, must be working out really well if Sally
was happy to leave her in charge of the yard already.
Carrie felt guilty about leaving her job, so it was a
relief that her replacement was a good one. Carrie
asked Sally if she knew of any horses that were
needing a home, as a companion for Bilbo, Sally said
she would ask around.

Carrie spent a happy few hours on Thursday at a
big equestrian and farm shop, stocking up with bits
for Bilbo and bits for the farm. She had a good list,
she knew she needed a new head collar for Bilbo, his
was fraying badly. The one she fell in love with was a
lovely soft leather, and not cheap. She decided to buy
a cheap one as well and keep the leather one for best.
She would like some new grooming brushes and
some special shampoo to keep Bilbo's coat healthy.
The brushes Bilbo had now were old and worn. The
concrete floors in the stables were hard and cold and
that worried her, so she bought some rubber mats
and arranged delivery, as they wouldn't fit in her car.
Under the straw, they would make a soft and warm

base layer. In time they would need loads of these mats but she would take whatever they had to start with. Maybe she should get some wood shavings for Bilbo's bedding too, instead of using the straw, that was what he was used to. She added that to the delivery order. Once she had chosen all the stuff from her list she browsed for an hour or two, just enjoying the smells of the leather tack and the stacks of horse feed. She might have made a few more impulse purchases, but nothing too expensive! Shopping for her horse was one time when she was tempted to be extravagant.

She enjoyed an early lunch, at a café, on the way home, then settled to some more cleaning for the afternoon. Caleb texted instead of Skyping that night, confirming that filming would soon be totally finished and he would be home the following evening. She was so happy she did a little dance around the room.

Just as Carrie was locking up to go to bed that night, her phone rang. She picked it up and saw it was Caleb, her heart leapt. Was he OK? It was only a couple of hours since they texted. She answered quickly. "Hi Lovely, this is a surprise call, are you all right?"

"Hi again Sweetie. I'm fine and sorry it's a bit late. I've just had a plea for help from my friend Babs at Mindon Rescue. She's the lady who is coming to give us advice on planning our sanctuary. They've just had a case, working with their local police, where thirty horses have to be removed from a farm, they are in very poor condition. She has spaces for some of them, including the ones needing urgent veterinary help, but she can't find space for the last ten or twelve. They need a home urgently and will need full veterinary check-ups asap. Do you think we can take them? Could you arrange a local vet to see them, if someone brings them to the farm? She doesn't think any of them are really sick, just thin and hungry, and needing treatment for worms. I'd love it if we could help – what do you think?"

"Ohh, poor ponies, of course we must help. Give me the lady's name and number and I'll talk with her now."

"I said I'd ring her back, so leave it with me, and I'll give her your number if that's OK? She was sounding stressed and exhausted so it'll be better if I do it, as she knows me. I'll tell her she has our full practical and financial support, if you are in agreement? Can we take any more horses, if it eases her

17

burden? Shall I tell her to call you first thing in the morning?"

"She can ring anytime she needs to. I'll take my phone to bed. I was checking some of the fields yesterday and they are ready to use. If she wants us to take more horses I'm happy to do it, especially if they just need food and not health care. If they are hungry a field might be the best place for them to be, on good grass, but I can have pens in the big barn ready first thing so whatever she advises, we have it. I'll say night night so you can get back to her now. Bye lovely."

Caleb whispered a sweet goodnight and ended the call. Carrie sat and thought for a moment, going through what she would need. She made a quick list of urgent items then decided to go to bed. It looked like she might need her sleep, tomorrow would be a big day.

Just as she was settling her phone rang. "Hi, is that Carrie? Sorry to ring so late but we're desperate to get these horses sorted. It's Babs from Mindon Rescue, by the way."

"Hi Babs, good to hear from you. We're ready to

help in any way we can. I have fields and pens ready, hay and straw in and no other animals here, in case there are any infectious illnesses or parasites. If they can go straight out to the fields, I can take up to twenty but if they need to be inside and have round the clock care probably ten would be the limit, as I'm here alone until tomorrow night. I'll find a vet in the morning. I'll drop Caleb's name into the conversation if I need to persuade them to take us on, that seems to work!"

"Oh Carrie, thank you so much, I really want to get them all out of that horrible place first thing in the morning. We've only got the really sick ones away so far today. There were three dead ones too, so sad. Our staff are exhausted. Our vets will find six well enough to travel. I'll use our lorry and get them down to you by 10am. If you can manage another six then they could be transported in the afternoon, assuming there are more that can stand the journey. With the ones here with us already, that would be all of them safe. I'll come with the first lot, and we can choose where to put them for the best. Outside is preferable, as it's what they're used to, but good grass might be too rich for them straight away, poor souls. If this sounds OK, I'll see you about 10am?"

"That all sounds good, we do have a few fields that have had cows on recently and the grass is quite short, that might be better for their digestion? You can see when you get here. We can pay for the diesel and help in other ways if you need it. Don't let lack of funds limit their care. I'll see you in the morning."

Carrie lay back on her pillow, feeling sad for the horses, but really excited to be able to help. For the first time, she really appreciated what good Caleb's money could do. Hopefully, this was the start of something wonderful.

Chapter 2

Arriving

Next morning, she was up at 6am. She had a quick slice of toast then went out to the big barn, that had animal pens at one end and the huge stack of hay and straw at the other. Some of the pens were about twelve foot square, suitable for one horse and some were bigger – nearer thirty by ten feet. She lugged bales of straw into six of the smaller ones. Next, she fetched a few bales of hay from the huge stack so they were readily available. Once she had checked the pens for any broken rails or sharp bits, she felt ready to welcome the horses. By this time it was nearly 8am so she went back to the house to try and find a local vet. She rang the first one of three listed that were pretty local. She didn't want to be too far from her vet if there was an emergency in the future. She hoped whichever vet she chose would form a good relationship with their sanctuary over time too.

"Good morning, Scarton Vets practice, how can

we help?"

"Good morning my name is Carrie Jones and I am calling from Cliff Top Farm, Santon. We've just moved here, with plans to turn the farm into a rescue centre. We didn't plan to take any animals for months, but a big case, undertaken by another rescue centre, has meant we've agreed to take between six and twelve horses as a matter of urgency today. The other centre is overwhelmed as there were thirty horses rescued from one site. They are all under-nourished and need checking over for any other problems. Do you have the capacity to take us on as a client immediately and send someone to assess and treat the horses today?"

"I'll need to speak to the practice manager, can I take your number please."

"Of course, but I do need a quick answer as, if you can't help, I must find another practice and get someone here by 10.30am if I can. Please can you give this your urgent attention? Thank you."

"I'll get back to you within 10 minutes. Bye for now."

Carrie found the numbers for the other nearby practices and fed the numbers into her phone, just in case. She made a cup of tea and fed Pickle while she waited for the call. It was less than 10 minutes later when the phone rang. "Hello Mrs Jones, It's Jan, the practice manager from Scarton vets here. I have looked at today's workload and I'm not sure we can help until this afternoon. I assume the horses coming are ones from the case reported on the news last night – it looked awful. Do you know what condition they're in, do they need time-critical care or would this afternoon be soon enough?"

"Unfortunately, until they arrive, I don't know much, but I do know any coming here will have been passed fit to travel, so I am guessing they are not critical. Can I ask you to send someone as soon as you can? If it's not until this afternoon at least we'll know help is coming?"

"I'll add you to our lists and talk with our vets to see if we can get to you any earlier. We'll need to officially register you as a client, but I'll send the paperwork with the vet. Good luck Mrs Jones and someone will be with you as soon as possible. Bye for now."

Carrie put the phone down and smiled to herself. "Well she sounded nice and efficient, let's hope they turn up earlier rather than later." Her next job should be to find a good farrier who can check and trim their feet, which were bound to be overgrown and unhealthy. She returned to her computer and found there was a farrier based in the village. She tried his number.

"Hello, Don Race, farrier."

"Hello Mr Race, I'm Carrie Jones, we are the new owners of Cliff Top farm. We have some horses arriving today, that are rescue cases, and are likely to have bad feet, can I book you to come and take a look as soon as possible? There will be somewhere between six and twelve animals and they will need ongoing care, as I suspect they will be here some time. A vet will hopefully be here this afternoon, if it would help you to talk with them."

"OK, I'm not working today but I can pop out this afternoon, see what needs doing, and trim any that can't wait a day or two. Would that suit you?"

"That would be brilliant, thank you. See you this afternoon then."

At 10am Carrie was waiting by the farm gate, looking out for a big livestock lorry. Babs had messaged to say they were on schedule. Carrie was nervous and excited, what a thrill to have their first animals arriving but how horrible that they had suffered, and some had died. She hoped to learn more about the case from Babs. She wished Caleb was home to see them get settled, it was the start of his dream, after all. She'd texted him earlier, to let him know the horses were on the way but he hadn't answered yet. He should be getting a flight at lunchtime and should be here tonight, not long now. At least she'd be kept busy once this lorry arrived. No time to get giddy with excitement today.

Just after 10am she heard the rumble of a big diesel engine approaching. The road past the farm was not used by lorries much, so she hoped it was them. As the lorry came into view, she could see it was a livestock wagon, and soon she could see a lady in the passenger seat waving. Carrie waved back and stepped to the side so the lorry could swing in through the gate. A window opened and Babs said, "Hi, Carrie, are we headed to those barns? If so, jump in."

Carrie climbed in beside Babs and the driver. "Hi

Babs, nice to meet you, how was the journey? Have the horses travelled well?"

"All good, poor loves. At least they are all trained horses, not young ones. They have probably travelled before and they're used to being handled by humans. I think we should pen them and check them all before we turn any out. Where should we park so they can go straight into the barn?"

"If we go to the end of the barn just past the house, you can reverse in and we'll unload straight into the pens. Are there six onboard this trip? If so, there are six single pens, I just need to spread some straw for them and put in some hay. Luckily the pens all have automatic drinkers which I checked last week, I must have had a premonition! Give me five minutes to spread the bedding before you lower the ramp."

"Good plan, I'll help."

Once the lorry was reversed into the barn Carrie and Babs jumped out and grabbed some straw bales. They shook the straw into six single pens and threw a section of hay in each for the horses to eat. They returned to the lorry just as the driver was lowering the ramp.

"They all have head collars on so we can lead them into the pens. I'll have to take the head collars back, though, as we need them for the next lot, do you have any?"

"Only two, from my horse, but we'll soon order more and I can't lead more than two horses at once anyway, I'll manage."

The horses came out of the lorry one at a time, each one being put in its own pen. They all looked filthy and thin but otherwise not really injured. There were two big horses that looked really skinny. The other four were much smaller, ponies really. Of the smaller ones three were mares, all thin, but not quite so bad as the bigger animals. They looked like hardy native breeds that do well on less food. They all had long and split hooves and their coats looked dull and dirty. The last to come out was a tiny Shetland gelding who was not really thin, but his poor feet were terribly overgrown and misshapen. How he was walking Carrie didn't know but he was managing quite well considering. "Oh my, Babs, do you ever get used to seeing animals in such a bad way?" asked Carrie. "How do you cope with it?"

Babs gave a sad smile. "No, you never get used to it, which is a good thing, it keeps you fighting the cause. It does get easier to see the animal underneath though – and see what they need to get better."

"Now they're eating and seem calm, shall we take a quick walk and see the fields. The ponies don't look so skinny, we could maybe give them the small paddock I was going to use for my own horse. Come and see what you think." Carrie and Babs headed to the small paddock.

"As you can see it's well sheltered by hedges and not too lush with grass, what do you think?"

"Perfect," said Babs, "the little mares should be fine here, maybe not the Shetland though – I suspect he might need even less grass, they tend to get fat very easily."

"What about the two bigger chaps, they look pretty poor. Could they go out here too?"

"If it were me, I think I'd start them in here for a few days then risk giving them a field of richer grass when they have got used to eating well again. They need all the goodness they can get, as long as their bellies can cope."

"So, it's just the Shetland we need to house then. I could bring him into the barn during the day and let him out with the others at night. That way he has less time to eat but still gets some freedom. If he still gets too fat, I can think again."

"Wow, we have them all sorted. What about bringing more? Do you have another field like this?"

"Yes, there are two more recently grazed ones but they're up on the cliffs and they're a lot bigger. I guess it depends on what you bring."

"How about using one of those for the two bigger horses? They are less likely to over eat so a big field won't hurt them. What about the vet, did you find one? They've all been assessed, very quickly, by our chaps but they could do with a full check-up."

"Hopefully one of the local practices is sending someone, but not until this afternoon. The village farrier is coming this afternoon too, to see what challenges he's facing. It's his day off but he didn't hesitate, hopefully a good sign for the future."

"You've done a great job with such short notice, thanks so much. It's such a relief to get them settled. Shall we check them again and then I'll head off back to the sanctuary. I'll ring you when I get back and let you know if we are bringing more this afternoon. Will you keep this lot inside until the Vet and farrier have been? Are you going to manage turning them out on your own afterwards?"

"Don't worry, I'll be fine, they don't look like they have the energy to be any bother!"

They walked back to the barn and found all the horses quietly devouring the hay they had given them. All except the little Shetland who had already finished his hay and was happily in the process of eating his straw bed. "OK," said Carrie laughing, "no wonder this one's not thin, he'll eat anything! I can see you're going to be trouble little man." She stroked his nose, which was now pushed through the bars, trying to see if they had food in their pockets. "I think he'll be out under those bars, if we're not careful, maybe he needs to come up to the house and go in a proper stable to be safe. He would happily eat all the grass on the farm if we let him, I think."

Babs laughed. "He is definitely a survivor, typical

Shetland"

"Do we know any of their names?" asked Carrie. "And am I allowed to ask why they were left in this state?"

Babs sighed. "It's a sad case and we don't know everything yet. The place where they were found used to be a riding school, up until a couple of years ago. The lady lived there alone and she slowly got rid of her staff and stopped giving riding lessons. She'd always been a bit of an eccentric horsewoman, and not overly popular locally. People felt she was deteriorating mentally, but she shut herself away with her horses and refused help. She was still buying food for the horses and herself and getting it delivered, so people drifted away, thinking she was just getting more eccentric. The horse feed was delivered to the yard gate and was disappearing. The food delivery from the supermarket was left by the back door each week, so the few people who might have worried, assumed she was just reclusive. Finally, this week, the feed merchant's driver got curious and went into the yard. He could smell something rotting and thought he should check. He found all thirty horses in a tiny paddock with no grass or feed. Luckily there was a self-filling water trough, that was dirty, but functioning. They were knee-deep in their own shit and three were dead, hence the smell. He called the police and they called us. The police searched the house and found the lady, quite happy, but totally out of her mind. She was as thin as the horses and seemed to have forgotten they existed! Somehow, she had been moving the feed delivery each week but just stashing it away in a shed and not giving it to the horses. According to the local bobby, she was convinced it was the 1970's and her husband would be home soon - he'd been dead for nearly 50 years! Poor lady, but poor, poor horses, victims of her mental deterioration.

So, we know nothing of their past, except that they must have been used in the riding school until a couple of years ago. They all act as if they've been used to people handling them. We'll ask local people, who may have ridden there before it closed, if they can tell us anything. Since the rescue was on the local news last night, we've already had calls from people who knew the horses. One was from someone who worked there until it closed. We should be able to piece together some history eventually. For now, though, your guess is as good as mine."

"Oh God, what a sad story. Poor woman, at least it

wasn't wilful neglect. Somehow it feels better knowing she was as much a victim as her horses. The thought someone would do this wilfully was driving me mad. They can all have temporary names until you find out more, so they feel wanted! This little chap's definitely going to need a cheeky name! Maybe Monkey would suit?"

"Ha ha – that sounds perfect! You can have fun learning their characters and naming them appropriately. I understand what you mean, about feeling better this case wasn't wilful neglect, but you'll have to get tougher, the wilful cases will come. When you see some of the things we've seen over the years, you lose faith in the human race pretty quickly. It's just as well meeting people like you and Caleb restores my faith, it keeps me sane! Anyway, we must get off and see what is happening at our sanctuary. I'll ring you if we have more to bring."

Carrie waved the lorry off and looked at the horses. At least they were getting food inside them now. The hay she'd used was last year's crop from the farm, this year's needed to 'mature' a few more weeks before she could start using it. Luckily the previous owner had shown her which was which. They had forty or so bales left of the old stuff so all was good. As she turned to go back to the house, she caught movement out of the corner of her eye. Monkey was reaching under the bars of his pen to steal the hay from the pony next door. He got an angry head swing and squeal from the bigger pony but he managed to grab a big mouthful as he retreated, unabashed. Carrie laughed and gave Monkey more hay of his own. She would find somewhere to put him where he could cause less trouble.

Chapter 3

Homecoming

Carrie walked back to the house and put the kettle on. It was only 11am, but she felt like she'd done a day's work, she guessed she had been stressing a bit. With her cup of tea and a slice of ginger cake, she sat at the kitchen table writing a list of things they would need, starting with a load more head collars. There was no way she could get to the farm shop to buy supplies today, but maybe if she phoned, they could deliver what she needed when they came with her previous purchases. She phoned her list through and they promised to deliver it all by the end of the day.

After placing the call Carrie took a moment to finish her tea and relax. She thought back to how emotionally shut down and lacking in confidence she had been a year ago, she patted herself on the back for how she had coped today, even under pressure. The love of a good man really helped, even if he was so far away, but she knew that she had finally healed inside. That was a wonderful feeling. When her husband, Matt, died she really believed she would never feel good or whole again. She didn't think she should allow herself to be happy anymore, he was dead so she should be dead inside. Looking back, that belief was rubbish, but at the time it was totally real and she lost two years of life living in her grief. Thank goodness for good friends and her inner spark that had slowly pulled her out of that time. And thank goodness for Caleb, seeing her inner spark and waiting for her to heal. She still missed Matt, but he was tucked safely in her heart, not ruling her life. She was free to enjoy this amazing life that had found her, even when she wasn't looking for it. She felt so lucky.

Just as she was slipping her yard boots back on, she heard a vehicle on the drive. She jogged around to the front of the house and waved. A man was just getting out of a beaten-up old transit van as she reached him.

"Hi love, I'm Don Race, the farrier, we spoke this morning."

"Hi Mr Race, thanks so much for coming on your day off, it's very kind of you."

They shook hands and he said, "Call me Don, Mr Race sounds so old! Now let's look at these horses and see if we can make them more comfortable."

They entered the barn and Don took a quick look at each animal. He moved around the horses with a firm but gentle manner, talking to them under his breath, picking up a hoof or two but mainly just assessing. Despite their recent trauma, all the horses were calm and docile around him. Carrie suspected she had lucked out and found a good farrier, even before he started any work. He came out of Monkey's pen last and said, "Well, they're not too bad considering. The little chap and one of the big bays will need more long-term remedial work but the rest should be fairly straightforward. In a few months you will never know they had problems, with any luck. Shall I start with the two worst ones and see how we get on?"

Carrie breathed a sigh of relief. "Yes please, it'll be good to see them walking better. I've just realised I have no small head collars yet. This all happened so fast I haven't been able to get anything in preparation. Can you manage the little chap if I plait up some bale string and make something?"

"Let's try him in the pen without tying him up, he may well stand happily. If not, I've got a couple of head collars in the van, they'll be too big but we'll manage."

Don fetched his toolbox and they both went into Monkey's pen. Don picked up a front hoof and had a good look. After a few moments he said, "OK, I know what I can achieve today, let's get started." He grabbed his hoof knife and pincers and got to work. Carrie stood by Monkey's head, ready to grab him if he misbehaved, but the little pony just stood there, almost enjoying his pedicure. Carrie hoped they would all be this calm. After ten minutes of careful trimming and assessing, Don stood to stretch his back muscles. "This could take some time and I'm gasping for a cuppa, any chance?"

Carrie laughed. "Typical farrier, here five minutes and expecting to be waited on! If you can manage this vicious beast by yourself, I'll go and put the kettle on." She made her way across to the house, grinning to herself.

As she rounded the corner of the house, she almost bumped into a woman hurrying away from the back door. "Oh, I'm so sorry, I'm Jane, the vet, come to look at some horses. I tried the front and back door but no one was in."

"Hi, I'm Carrie, and thanks for coming so early, I was just coming in to make tea for the farrier, would you like a cup?"

"Ooh yes please, I haven't stopped all morning. Can I come in and drop off the paperwork the practice sent you, then we can go and see the horses?"

"Sounds like a plan," said Carrie, "come on in. Do you know Don Race, the farrier? I phoned him because he is the nearest, he seems really nice."

"Yes, he's a good chap. I heard he wasn't working much, since his wife died, maybe he's getting back to it now though, that's good news." Carrie's heart went out to Don, she knew that pain so well. "I think the tea is brewed, let's carry the drinks over to the barn and see how it's going."

They reached the barns to find Don still hard at work with Monkey, trimming the back feet now. "I found an abscess in this back foot, it wasn't deep or big and it has drained nicely. Maybe now Jane's here she could give him a jab of antibiotic? I don't think it needs a poultice as I cut most of the pocket of infection away as I was trimming."

Jane was in beside him now and looking at the hoof. Monkey sniffed her and snuffled in her pocket. "Hello little one, you're a sweetie," said Jane, giving him a stroke. "I think you're quite right Don, looks like most of the problem is gone, but I'll jab him just in case, when you've finished."

Jane started checking the horses at the other end of the pens while Carrie told her what she knew of their past. Don was listening too, whilst he trimmed, and he said, "I remember that riding school, she had a good reputation once, most of the local kids went there. Before I married, I lived in the next village. Such a shame no one knew she needed help."

Jane gave each horse a thorough check, listening to their hearts and breathing, taking temperatures and taking bloods to check for any invisible problems. She examined their coats for parasites and gave each horse a dose of medicine to kill any parasitic worms they might have in their guts. She had a good feel over each horse's body to check for lumps, bumps or cuts. Finally, she checked their feet and discussed her findings with Carrie and Don.

"To be honest, apart from their thinness and general poor condition, I can't find too much wrong with them. One of the big chaps does have a very slight heart murmur, but that's not unusual when they are so underweight, it usually rights itself as they get fatter. We should recheck him in a week or so, to be sure it's not getting worse. Mostly their weight and feet are the biggest problems. I have wormed them all and given them a general booster with multivitamins and other good stuff in. I will leave you with sachets of gut improver which should kick start the gut bacteria and help them cope with more food. I would say hay or plenty of fibrous grazing will get them right quicker than anything. Give the big ones some high protein, high-fat feed once they are managing the grass well, that should build them up a bit quicker. If you can turn them out on good grazing, nature will do most of the work for you. As you know, just look for signs of poor gut health like the squits or any discomfort. Call straight away if you are worried."

"Wow, thank you, that's really good news. I can get them out on some grass straight away, once Don is finished. There may be some more arriving from the same place this afternoon, can we book you to come back once we know?"

"Yes, just ring my mobile, I'd like to stay involved. If you ring the surgery, they'll just send whoever's free. Here's my number. I'll see you later even if no more horses appear, I'd like to see them again once they are out on the grass. If you need me urgently before then just ring."

"Thanks so much Jane, how long will the blood test results take?"

"Some tests are in-house, so I might even have those later, some have to be sent away, so they will be a few days. See you later on. Bye Don, if you find anything I need to see, just let me know and I'll look later. Good to see you out and about again." She left with a wave.

As Jane left, Carrie looked at Don and saw him wiping his eyes hastily. He saw her looking and bent to his work quickly. Within ten minutes Don had finished Monkey's feet and was coming out of the pen. "He'll need regular trimming for a few months to get his feet back to a normal shape, I can't do it all at once or I'll make him very sore, but he should feel better already, with that abscess gone and lots trimmed off his little hooves. Let's look at the big guy with the very cracked feet next."

It was quickly obvious that the bigger horse was not going to stand still to be trimmed like Monkey had. Don went and found a head collar and Carrie held him still. Once Don got to work the horse slowly relaxed and stilled. Within half an hour he was finished and the news was good. None of the cracks were as deep as they looked and trimming the hooves back had got rid of most of them. "He'll do for now, I can do more in a couple of weeks. The ground's not too dry so they should improve and not crack further."

Don worked his way through the other four animals, trimming and rasping their feet until they all looked as normal as possible. As he worked Carrie chatted away about their plans for the farm. She told Don that she would love him to be their regular farrier if he would consider it. He seemed hesitant and didn't actually commit. Carrie wondered if he was grieving still and having trouble with committing to anything. She remembered months of that feeling, being too scared to take on challenges in case she messed up and got upset. She decided she should tell him about her past, maybe it would help him, to know she had been there too.

"Do you know, I'm so happy now, but right up to this time last year I was a total mess. I was grieving for my husband, who was killed in a car crash, I was so low. It is hard to believe, that, within three years of his death, I am now starting this wonderful new adventure. I still love and miss him, but I realised I don't need to live my life in the shadow of his death anymore. I even have a new fiancé now. I never thought I'd be OK with loving again, but I know in my heart that my husband would approve. It does get easier you know, how long has it been?"

"How did you know? Jane, I suppose. Shit, and then you saw me crying like a baby. Thanks for bringing it up!" Don looked uncomfortable and cross. "I only came here because I thought you wouldn't know, being new here. Everywhere I go people look at me with pity – or avoid me! I hoped, here, I could just be normal and not the grief-stricken husband."

Carrie looked at her feet. "Oh Don, I'm so sorry, I hoped knowing I've been through similar grief might help you. I didn't mean to make you feel bad. I really do understand though. Everyone treats you like you are some fragile, broken person, when you are trying so hard not to be that person – it sucks. People don't know what to say and they get it wrong, not because they don't care but because they don't know how you feel. Most of the time **you** don't know how you feel, you just want to pretend you are whole and normal and get through the day."

She looked at Don again, his anger had softened, he said, "Wow, you do understand. I think it's worse being a man in a tough physical occupation, you're not supposed to have emotions on show in my job. When people think you're broken they avoid you. I lost so many customers, to other farriers, over the first few months. Even though I was working, no one wanted me around. I made them uncomfortable just by being quiet, not even crying or anything. No one could see past the grief and see it was still me. I felt like I had lost so much more than my wife – I had lost everything, lost me."

Carrie, on impulse, stepped forward and gave Don a big long hug. "You are still in there Don, you will find yourself again soon. Please believe that you deserve to be happy again. Your wife will always be with you, you don't have to hang on to her by being

sad. I'm sure she would never want that for you."
She led him to a hay bale to sit down.

   "I can't think ahead at all," he said, "the thought
of moving on scares the shit out of me. I just work
when I can and spend the rest of the time sitting
crying, and thinking of her. I can't even remember
her properly, it's like losing her again, every day. If I
do remember her - I cry - the good times have been
stolen from me, because they don't make me feel
good now." Don was crying openly, Carrie felt
herself crying with him.

   "If it will help, I can explain what I found
happened to me. You will get her memory back
when you no longer need her. You will always love
her but when you stop needing her, you will be able
to function in the present. I thought I would lose
Matt if I stopped needing him, in fact, I finally got
him back, in my heart and in my memory. No one
can change what happened but you can change how
you live going forward. Surround yourself with good
people who you can trust to see you cry. Let yourself
fail sometimes, but, move forward. Try to fill your
life with new things that take up your time and
mind. One day you will look back and realise the bad
times weren't failures, just part of the journey. Come

46

here and talk to me whenever you need to, I do understand. I spent two years crying – it's OK to cry, but it's OK to stop. Help it stop by not giving yourself time to brood. You are always welcome here, whether you are happy or crying, let this be a safe place to be yourself, tears and all.

Don looked at her with gratitude. "I can't say I understand exactly what you mean, but I can feel that you understand what's happening to me. You have no idea what that means to me. No one, even my close family, really understand. They think if they care for me I should be OK, so they do, and I'm not. I have come so close to taking too many pills or sinking to the bottom of a bottle of whisky. It's letting my family down that stops me. Talking to you, now, as someone who has gone through it too, makes me feel safe for the first time since........" Don dissolved into quiet tears again.

Carrie put her arm around his shoulders and let him cry. If she could help him in the way Sally and her house-mates had helped her, she would be so happy.

After a few minutes, Don gave her a watery smile and stood up. "Your new fiancé is a lucky man

Carrie, I hope he knows that. I'm not coming on to you here, I'm being serious, you are amazing. You don't know me from Adam but you've sat here and shared your darkest moments, just to try and help me. You are stuck with me as a farrier now, I have a debt to repay!"

"No debt," said Carrie. "Just pay it forward, that's what I'm doing. But I'd be so happy if you'll care for our horse's feet. I meant what I said though, come here whenever it gets too much for you in the real world. I've found out that this farm is a peaceful and healing little place over the last few weeks. I'm sure it could help you, and I can always make tea and listen. When you meet Caleb, you'll see he has a big heart too, he will welcome you."

"Will he mind that you hugged me and let me cry all over you?"

"Not if he's the man I think he is – know he is. But I will explain it carefully, he's been away for months and I don't want him getting the wrong idea!"

"You must miss him like mad, you can't have been together long before he went away. When is he due back?"

"Right about now!" boomed a loud and deep voice from behind them.

Carrie swung around with a squeal and rushed into Caleb's arms. He hugged her to him and kissed the top of her head. She looked up, a little wary, but he just kissed her passionately and deeply. When he pulled away, finally, Carrie whispered, "are we OK?"

He smiled at her, tucked her under his arm and held his hand out to a very uncomfortable and worried looking Don.

"Hi, I'm Caleb, the fiancé, and I must apologise for eavesdropping on your private conversation with Carrie. I'm afraid I arrived just as you were hugging and, while I trust Carrie totally, my manly pride had to know I wasn't seeing what I thought I was seeing. Rather than follow my instincts and kill you, I listened in for a moment. I'm sorry I intruded on your grief, but rest assured, the alternative would not have been pretty! Now, instead of being angry and hurt, I am just immensely proud of my beautiful partner for reaching out to you, and I hope we can be friends..........?"

Carrie breathed a sigh and relaxed as she watched

Don's face. His expression went from horror, to embarrassment, to anger and briefly stopped on recognition. Shock and disbelief followed, underpinned with a huge amount of relief! It was an entertaining display.

"Bloody Hell! You didn't say he was **that** Caleb, I need a sit down. Are we really OK mate, Carrie may just have saved my life in the last half hour, the last thing I want is to cause you both any strife. Hitting on someone else's girl was absolutely the last thing on my mind today." Don plonked himself down on the bale of hay and held his head in his hands. Carrie suspected there were tears again, but she needed to talk to Caleb.

She quietly pulled Caleb a few steps away and whispered. "You do really understand what was happening, don't you? He's caught in the same cycle of grief I was for years, I needed to help him. The hug was just to comfort him, nothing more."

Caleb looked deep into her eyes and said, "I trust you and I trust your judgement, I love that you reached out to him, and I heard enough to know you are an amazing, generous, caring person. I feel proud of you and ashamed that I had even a second of doubt. I love you, Carrie."

"Oh Caleb, I'm so glad you're home, I'm done being strong for today, can I lean on you for a bit? I love you so much." They kissed again then turned to comfort Don, together.

By the time they returned to Don he was grinning sheepishly and watching them. "You look happier," said Carrie, touching his shoulder.

"I'm so happy to see I haven't messed up your relationship, I thought I'd never be able to show my face here again. Caleb, thank you for being so understanding, I'm not sure I would have been in your situation."

Caleb replied, "Hey, we're cool, any friend of Carrie's is a friend of mine, just remember she **is** mine and we'll be fine!"

"No worries there mate, I don't think I could compete with Mr Caleb Kirkmichael even if I wanted to."

Carrie laughed and said, "If we are all done with the testosterone talk, can we head to the house for a cup of tea? I'm exhausted."

"Hang on, aren't you going to introduce me to our new guests, or did you think I flew home overnight, in economy class, on the last seat available just to see you?" quipped Caleb.

"Oh my days, I'd totally forgotten you haven't seen them, come and meet Monkey and friends. Then you can explain how you are home nearly twelve hours early, not that I'm complaining! Don could you tell Caleb what you found with their feet as we go along – you can explain it better than me." They went along the line of horses, with Don explaining what he'd done in each case and what they would need going forward. When they reached little Monkey, Caleb just melted.

"Aww who's this little fella, he's soooo cute! His feet look a bit strange, is he going to be OK?" Don reassured Caleb that Monkey's hooves would recover with a bit of help. "How come he's got a name and the others haven't?" Caleb asked.

Carrie explained, "I named him this morning, he's quite a cheeky chap and Monkey fit the bill. He's made his presence known ever since he arrived. The others are more polite and haven't pushed themselves forward for naming yet. Tea, now, while I tell you all about them."

"I'll leave you two to it then, you'll have lots to catch up on," said Don.

"Thanks for all you've done Don. Would you come back later if more horses arrive?" asked Carrie.

"Just ring me if you need me. I'll be at home, not brooding, I promise. I'll be planning how to get my life moving on again!"

Caleb added "Please come back soon and chat with Carrie, even if the horses don't need your help. I'm sure sharing your experiences will help both of you to heal. I can make myself scarce for an hour or so."

Don headed for his van saying. "You are both amazing people, and I will be back – I haven't had the courage to ask for an autograph yet!" He went off grinning and feeling like a weight was slowly lifting.

Chapter 4

Discovering

Caleb and Carrie walked back to the house, arm in arm, and made that cup of tea. Caleb explained that they finished filming quickly and he went straight to the airport to find an earlier flight. He was at the airport when he texted her and almost boarding when the call came in from Babs. He hadn't told her about being on an earlier flight as he wasn't sure he would get a seat at first, and later it was all a massive rush to get the calls finished as he boarded. They squeezed him onto the overnight flight, in the last seat on the plane. He had stopped for breakfast at Heathrow then finally found a cab to bring him all the way home. The cab journey had been horrendous , with the usual road works and accidents causing long delays. He was exhausted, but happy now he was home.

They were sat in the kitchen, drinking tea and chatting, when Carrie's phone bleeped with a message. It was Babs

Hi Carrie, sorry for the delay, we are on our way to you with four more horses. Sadly, when we got back to our sanctuary, two of the really poorly horses had just been put down by our vets. They were both elderly and had underlying conditions that meant they were deteriorating fast, and in pain. Thankfully the rest are responding well. With two spare places here now, I only need to bring these four to you and we are sorted. We will be there about 4.30pm by my reckoning. Hope the others are all OK? Babs x

Carrie showed Caleb the text and checked the time. They probably had about half an hour before Babs arrived. "I need to get the first lot of horses put out in their fields before the next lot arrive. You sit here and rest and I'll get that sorted. I only have two head collars so I'll just make a few trips. Babs and I decided where they should go earlier."

Caleb looked at Carrie and grinned. "I love seeing you all fired up and confident, I can see you've done some serious healing while I've been away. I'm coming to help, there's no way I'm missing those horses seeing grass for the first time in ages. And there's no way I'm letting you out of my sight now

I'm home!"

Carrie was secretly very happy with that, so they headed out again, with Bilbo's new head collars, to turn the horses out. They led the two bigger horses out to the field near the cliffs and carefully let them go. They seemed a bit confused at first and just stood by the gate. After a few seconds, they took a couple of steps, then their heads were down and they were grazing like their life depended on it.

The smaller ponies went to Bilbo's little paddock and Monkey went with them for now, until they could decide how to keep him from overeating. When all four ponies were together, they squealed and bucked as they galloped around the paddock, so happy to be together and have food. They soon settled, and their heads never left the grass after that. It was such a wonderful sight to see them all eating peacefully, after what they'd been through. Carrie and Caleb just stood and watched for a while.

As they returned to the barn, a lorry turned into the drive. It was Babs with the next load of horses. Carrie rushed to clean up four of the pens for them and add more hay. Caleb walked down the drive to meet the lorry. Once the lorry had reversed in, Caleb and Babs jumped down from the cab chatting away and the driver came around to the back to let the ramp down. "What have we got this time?" Carrie asked the driver. "Did they travel OK again?"

He smiled. "You have four cobs, all skinny and needing a hoof trim but all sensible and quiet on the lorry. They've had a more thorough vet check than the others and have been wormed this morning. Apart from their weight and feet, they seem good. Two of them have rain scald quite badly but the vet has put cream on for today, they will need more each day until it settles down."

They opened the inner gates on the lorry and started unloading the horses. The first two off were a pair of big black and white cobs with lovely long hairy feathers on their legs. Both had a white cream spread on their backs. They were almost identical, even their black markings were similar in shape. Their feathers were coated in muck and their hooves were long and cracked but their eyes were bright as they looked around the barn.

As they put the first two in neighbouring pens, Caleb and Babs unloaded the last two. These were smaller cobs, one grey and one black. Both looked in a similar condition to the others, except they had no rain scald. The driver continued his comments. "The grey is quite old, but seems healthy, apart from the obvious. The little black Fell pony is younger, maybe seven or eight, and again in fair shape. The piebalds are around ten years old and we've been told they have pulled a cart as a pair, as well as been ridden individually. They are well matched, I bet they looked good pulling a cart together. We are slowly getting more history trickling in from locals, we know all of these one's names and the names of both of the big ones from earlier."

"Can we write a list of their names, I'm not sure I'll remember them otherwise. Monkey will be Monkey whatever his real name is, but the others should keep their names. I'll start a file for each one on the computer, so I remember any treatment they have or when they need the farrier again." Carrie's head was working overtime trying to keep all the details together. She knew she needed to get it all written down before she slept, it would be gone by the morning. She took a pen out of her pocket and jotted down the names the driver gave her.

Caleb put his arms around her from behind as the driver went back to the lorry. "I'm back now, you don't have to be organised all by yourself, we'll work out a system tonight and get it all recorded. You have done an amazing job today Carrie, thank you for taking this on so willingly."

"I've loved every minute of it, and it's not over yet. Are you sure you don't need to go and rest Caleb, I am worried you'll be exhausted."

He nuzzled her neck with his long stubble and whispered, "Are you worried I won't have the energy to satisfy you later? Don't worry, I've been storing up that kind of energy for weeks!"

Carrie gave him a kiss and a wink. She said, "The thought never crossed my mind. I might be the one who's too tired, it's been a long day."

He grinned and replied, "I know a cure for tiredness, I'll show you later!"

"Hey love-birds, we need to get away now, if there's nothing else you need? Have you got a plan where to put these ones?" Babs was standing by the lorry laughing at the two of them.

"Sorry Babs," said Caleb, "It's been weeks since I

got to hold my girl. We have everything we need, I think. I expect this lot can go out with the big ones on the cliffs. Or maybe the ones needing cream on can stay nearer the house for now. We'll sort them out when the farrier has been. It's been great seeing you again Babs, we will catch up on the phone tomorrow, when we will let you know how this lot are settling in."

Carrie and Caleb waved them off, then had a closer look at the new horses. Carrie texted both the vet, Jane and Don to ask them to come and see the four of them, just to be sure all was well. As with the previous six, the four cobs were happily eating their hay and seemed very settled already. They decided to leave them in peace for a while and returned to the house. Whilst Carrie made them some beans on toast, Caleb had a good look around the house. When he came back to the kitchen he gave Carrie a huge hug. "What was that for?" she asked. "Not that you need a reason, just curious."

"You've worked so hard in here, the whole place feels so much like home. I love the bedroom, the colour and the new bed, I can't wait for the test drive!"

"I've loved making a nest for us, is that weird? It made me feel like you were here with me, in a way. I felt a bit limited, as I know it will all change soon, but it was still lovely to do it. I didn't know what colours you like or anything, I hope the lilac is bearable?"

"I might have chosen it myself, it feels relaxing and soft. You know me better than you think."

"We must look at the stables later, they are really amazing. I've been making a nest for my 'other man' too!"

"As long as it's outside, I'm OK with that," he laughed.

Just as they had finished their beans on toast, they heard yet another vehicle arriving. Caleb made Carrie stay sitting down and went out to look. He returned after ten minutes, with a delivery note and a grin on his face. "Who's been spending all our money on girlie accessories again?" he joked. "I got them to drop the whole lot in the machinery barn, we can sort it tomorrow. You are the least girlie shopper I've ever met, not a single bath bomb or lipstick, just a load of rubber mats and some horse stuff!"

Within half an hour, Don and Jane both arrived to look over the four newcomers. Jane took bloods, gave them the jabs she gave the others, had a quick listen to their hearts and checked their temperatures. She and Don discussed their hooves and Don got trimming. Carrie noticed that Jane was watching Don work quite intently and she heard them chatting away and laughing. She quietly grabbed Caleb and whispered, "We're going for a walk."

He looked confused but happily followed. "Where are we going?" he asked.

"Anywhere we're not playing gooseberry, I think there might be the start of something wonderful happening in there."

"Really? I don't think Don is anywhere near that stage yet, from what I saw earlier," said Caleb.

"No, but if he's as dense as I was, he never will be without a push. I think Jane might be pushing, just a little, in there. She was watching him as you watched me in the restaurant that first night. Every time I looked at you, you seemed to be looking at me, it was weird but kind of nice. It got me thinking that maybe I did still have a pulse, that I could still appreciate a hottie like you. It was a baby step, but it got me thinking. Let's hope Jane can get Don thinking."

"Did I tell you, you're amazing?" Caleb held her tight and kissed her deeply. They spent a few happy moments exploring each other's mouths, then Carrie giggled and said, "We need to cool it a bit, we have loads to do before we can 'test drive' the bed!"

Eventually, they made their way back to the barn and found Don packing up. Jane was still there, chatting as he worked. "All done here," said Don. "They'll just need checking and re-shaping every couple of weeks, like most of the others. I'll come and check Monkey in a week, and the rest will be fine for a fortnight."

Jane added, "Nothing to report from me, as you suspected, they just need food and Don's regular attention, unless anything changes with them. Do you have enough of the cream for the rain scald?"

Carrie answered, "Yes to the cream, it came with them. And good to know all is well so far. Did you get any results from the bloods?"

"I don't have any results from earlier but they'll

get done tomorrow and I'll let you know what's what. I don't expect to find much, but better safe than sorry."

Caleb said, "Thank you both so much for all your work today, it was short notice and you have both gone above and beyond with your time. Can we invite you both in for a cuppa before you go?

Jane said she had to get home, "I should've been home a while ago, Mum's dogs will have their legs crossed, but thanks for the offer. If you can get the paperwork back to the practice, they'll send a bill and register you ready for next time. Bye for now and good luck with the horses, if you need me anytime just call, you have my mobile number. Bye Don." Jane went off to find her car.

Don said, "I'd love a cuppa some other time, and a chat Carrie, if that's OK? But you two must be desperate to be alone, after all this time, so I'll shoot now and see you soon. Thanks, Carrie, for reaching out to me and making me feel I'm not alone, no one else has managed that in all these months. And thanks Caleb for not killing me earlier!" Caleb just smiled and handed Don a piece of paper.

Don unfolded the paper and laughed, he showed Carrie, it said:

To Don

With thanks for all your work today, and in the future. Thanks, also, for not trying to steal my girl!

All the best

Caleb Kirkmichael

Caleb had signed it with a big, bold, autograph type signature.

Don was still chuckling to himself as he got in his van and drove away.

Carrie reached up and kissed Caleb. "Thank you," she whispered.

Chapter 5

Rediscovering

Carrie and Caleb led the two smaller cobs up the track to the cliff field. They'd already put the two big black and white cobs in with the three little mares, and checked Monkey wasn't eating himself silly. As they walked, they enjoyed the fading light. The sky had a lovely orange tinge as the sun went down. "I can't believe I'm finally here," Caleb said, "I've dreamed of this day for so long. Having you here, to share it with me, has made it so much better than my dream. We'll be so happy, I just know it's where we're meant to be, does that sound daft?"

"Not at all. I've been here two weeks and I've felt exactly the same. There's something almost magical about this place, it's taken care of me and made me feel so safe. I'm not used to being alone but I never felt worried, even in the middle of the night. I almost didn't want to leave to go shopping, it's been wonderful. It feels even more wonderful now you're home to share it with me."

The horses were walking slowly and grabbing mouthfuls of grass as they went. There was no hurry now, so they let them amble and graze. There were no sounds but the crying of the gulls overhead and the munching of the horses, perfect. When they finally reached the cliff field, the two bigger horses came to the gate, calling for their friends. They let the little cobs go and watched as they greeted the other horses, then started to graze. Once they knew they were all settled, Caleb said, "Shall we walk to the cliff edge? It's not far." They followed the track beside the field and soon found themselves on the cliff path.

When Caleb's lawyer had been doing the conveyancing for the farm, he discovered there was a public right of way along the cliff edge. Caleb had not been concerned, the fields were well fenced and the path was mostly used by serious walkers, as it was miles from anywhere. Now they wandered along the path, enjoying the view as the sun went down. They came to a wide flat area and realised this was where they got engaged, all those weeks ago. They sat in the long grass and reminisced about their relationship so far.

"I feel so happy now, it seems surreal, looking back. I feel like a different person, so much more serene, more confident. I can't believe I'd lost so much of myself after Matt died. I didn't realise at the time, but I wasn't me at all. I feel me again now, thanks to you Caleb."

Caleb hugged her as they sat, "You were always there, just like you told Don earlier, you showed moments of your true sparkle even then. There were just times when the clouds came down, and you couldn't find your sparkle. I could see it from the first time I looked in your eyes. When you suddenly burst into tears that first evening, as we ate, it was like something clouded over inside you. I saw it coming and didn't know what to do, or why it happened, I just knew I wanted to make it stop, to put the sparkle back. I remember finding myself hugging you before I knew what I was doing. That was the moment I realised, you were already in my soul. Something switched inside me when I touched you, and I finally understood all the romance films and love stories. I'd never felt anything like it before. I liked women, I really liked women, but I liked them for what I got out of them. Not just sex, but company and softness, and sex, mainly sex, now I look back. God, I was a prick. I was a polite and thoughtful prick, but still a prick. I never gave anything of myself, I just took. As soon as I met you, I knew I'd been missing something. Something huge. I wanted to give you my whole self, even if you couldn't give me anything back. I was scared to even contact you after that first night, in case I messed up and came on too strong. I knew you were still healing and weren't ready for love. That time you texted me, at the awards ceremony, I wanted to stand up and tell the world, 'she's thinking of me!' I was so happy. The riding lesson for Simon and me was my bright idea. It was mainly so I could see you without letting my feelings show. Simon needed the lesson, I knew I didn't, but it was a way to be with you for a while. When we sat on that beach and I finally blurted out my feelings, my heart was breaking, I knew you weren't ready, but I knew you were close. I knew I was going to have to go back to the States for months. I tortured myself with images of coming back here, to find you had found someone else to love. I had to tell you, but I thought you would reject me, or feel too much pressure and back off. It's the hardest thing I've ever done."

"Oh Caleb, I think I knew, deep down, from that first night too. I just never thought it could happen, you were an international film star for Pete's sake. I was so broken still, I never thought I could love someone new. Matt's death had become my excuse for never risking myself again. I had huge feelings for you but I explained them away, or just plain denied them to myself. I dreamt of you, I fantasised about you, but I couldn't let myself believe it was real. To be fair, you were so out of my league, it was easy to dismiss my feelings as a star struck crush. Because you were keeping away, I assumed that I was alone in my feelings, that I was just a bit messed up. I'm so glad you told me that day. I was healing fast and I would have moved on, thinking I needed a real man, not the fantasy that was you. I would have settled for someone safe and available, thinking I couldn't have you. You were so brave, and thank goodness you were. We are meant to be here together, with loads of animals to save and enjoy."

Carrie reached for Caleb's lips and kissed him soundly. He responded and their kiss deepened. All the passion and longing inside them took hold. Caleb's hands were everywhere, stroking and exploring. Carrie was tugging at his shirt and lifting it over his head. Caleb's hands were at her back and unhooking her bra, removing it and her shirt in one rough move. Carrie's hands stroked his bulging jeans and he let out a deep, guttural moan. He undid his flies as she stood and yanked her trousers and panties off. Within seconds, he was inside her as they rolled on the grass, skin to skin, touching and panting, as they both rushed headlong towards their release.

As soon as their passion began to calm, they looked at one another in amused awe. "Wow, that came out of nowhere," giggled Carrie, "I've never made love on a cliff before!"

"Not exactly what I'd call 'making love', far too desperate and quick. But amazing! I had great plans to gently seduce you tonight, taking my time and loving you like you deserve. Maybe I fantasised about it once too often through the day! I want to say I'm sorry for having no control, but I'm not, that was sooooo hot," laughed Caleb.

"I don't remember complaining." She grinned. "We have all night to take it slow, in fact, we have the rest of our lives, so no pressure! Just having you here is enough, anything else is a bonus. And that was super hot, but I'm getting dressed before we offend any local hikers." Carrie laughed as she retrieved her clothes, whilst trying to hide in the long grass, just in case.

They walked slowly back to the house, holding hands and enjoying the peace. The kettle went on as soon as they entered the back door. Carrie was amazed how normal it felt, just peaceful, and like they'd been here for years. She realised she should have planned a meal but decided a takeaway would have to do. They searched the net for a local food place but found nothing nearby. Caleb phoned a taxi company, asked if they would pick up a Chinese meal in town and deliver it to them. He paid for the taxi, and the meal, over the phone and was told it would be with them in an hour. Carrie was amazed, she didn't even know you could do that, she tried not to think how much it cost. While they waited, Carrie showered and found some pyjamas to wear. They chatted as they ate and started to work out a record system for the horses. Once that was done, they just lay on the sofa together and relaxed.

Chapter 6

Monkeying

Carrie woke slowly, feeling warm and cosy, but not quite normal. She stirred a bit and opened her eyes.

"Hi beautiful," said a voice that made her smile.

"Hi Caleb. Have you been awake long?"

"Only about half an hour, and I was in no hurry to move."

As she woke further, Carrie slowly realised where they were. "Oh my goodness, we're still on the sofa, what time is it?"

"About 8.30am – we must have both been exhausted, I don't remember waking up once during the night."

"Why didn't you wake me before, you must be uncomfortable, I can feel your arm under me?"

"I've been enjoying watching you sleep, you looked so cute and peaceful. I must admit, some blood supply to my arm would be nice, so maybe we should move soon?"

Carrie laughed and rolled off the sofa to give him some space.

He rubbed his arm and sat up. "So much for test driving the new bed. I can't believe we both passed out like that, all our plans for hot sex forgotten. We must be getting old!"

"Speak for yourself granddad, I'm in my prime." she laughed. "It was a long day yesterday though, for both of us. Oh, the horses, I must check them, I hope they are all OK, I need to move Monkey too – he'll be overeating." She jumped up and headed for her boots by the back door.

Caleb laughed. "Slow down petal, we can do them together, are you really going out in your Pjs?"

"Great to the help, and yes to the Pjs, but we

should do them now, I need to know they're all OK, so I can relax and enjoy a cup of tea."

Caleb smiled and fetched a set of keys, "I'll drive up and check the cliff field, you wander round the back and check the others. Monkey will live for another hour on the grass, we'll make a plan for him after breakfast, when we can think straight."

They headed off to do their checks, after a quick kiss. Carrie rounded the back of the courtyard and had a quick head count as she approached the paddock. All standing up, all eating, all peaceful, she breathed a sigh of relief. As she went through the gate, six heads came up from the grass and looked at her. Monkey whinnied and came over to check her pockets. She looked him over for any injuries or problems, he looked fine. She wandered around the others, talking gibberish and checking them over. Everyone looked really good. She could swear their bellies were looking rounder already. She knew getting the weight back on their rumps and shoulders would be a longer process. All the time she was wandering around the others, Monkey was following her with interest. "You are a nosy little chap aren't you? Are you checking I'm not giving the others treats and missing you out?" Monkey just nuzzled her pocket hopefully.

Carrie wandered back to the house, happy that all was well. Caleb arrived back a few minutes later, to report that all was well on the cliffs too. Time for that cup of tea.

After a shared shower, that had little to do with getting clean and a lot to do with reacquainting, they sat at the kitchen table, reviewing their records for the horses. "So, let me get this straight," said Caleb, "we have a name for the big boy with the cracked feet, he's Sonny, the other big one is Jaffa. The little grey cob is Cloud and the black one is Noddy. In the other field we have Monkey, who we need to move in a minute, the two big piebald cobs, who are Bud and Carl, do you think they are named after lagers by any chance? We also have the three little chestnut mares, who don't have names yet. Have I missed anyone?"

"No, that's it," said Carrie. "Should we give the mares names, or wait and see if Babs learns more? I feel sad they don't even have names. And where shall we put Monkey? I think in the stables, here in the yard would be best. He was trying to get out of the pen in the barn and he's almost small enough to succeed. I'd hate him to get stuck or something."

76

"How about we do some fencing and build him a big pen in the courtyard. He could go inside the old open cart shed if he wants shelter. Otherwise he can trundle around and exercise a bit without any grass to fatten him up. We'll be in and out all day so he won't be too bored. He can go out with the others at night."

"That's a great idea, but maybe just give him the back half of the courtyard, as we want access to the back door and the stables while he's in. We can fence off half of it, he won't be in the way and we won't get frisked for treats every time we come in or out!"

"We have good problem solving skills between us, I love it," smiled Caleb, "but I have no idea how to build a fence on a concrete yard. Who should I hire to do it?"

Carrie laughed, "I'm sure we can work it out without a fencing contractor, save that for the big jobs. What about Mr Quaggan, the farmhand? I think he'll be back from his holiday, shall we ring and see if he's decided to work with us? I bet he could knock up a fence in five minutes."

"I'll phone him now, it'll be great to have help

with all the ideas running round in my head. I'm keen, but not very experienced at practical stuff. I bet he can teach me loads. His knowledge of this farm will help us so much."

Caleb grabbed a phone and stood outside to call Mr Quaggan, while Carrie washed their breakfast dishes. When he came back in he was grinning, "He wants to start on Monday, I told him about the fence for Monkey and asked him to order whatever he thinks we need. He'll get the builders merchant to ring me, to pay for it over the phone. Hopefully we can get cracking as soon as it arrives. I told him to order more than we need, there are bound to be other fencing jobs sooner or later. He didn't say, but I think he's more than ready to get back to work, maybe his wife's a bit of a dragon?" They giggled at the thought.

The rest of Saturday was spent lazily sorting out this and that, and generally relaxing. Jane phoned to say all the blood test results so far were clear, but there were a handful outstanding. Caleb phoned Babs to report all the horses were well and to see how her lot were. She had talked more with the ex-member of staff from the riding school. She had given names for the three chestnut mares, although she had no idea which was which, without seeing them. She did say she thought the old lady had the horses micro-chipped, so a vet could probably read the chips and get some more details. All Babs' horses were doing fine, she sounded a lot more relaxed. With an agreement to visit in a couple of weeks, when things were a bit less hectic, Babs sent love to Carrie and rang off. Carrie texted Jane and asked if she could bring a microchip reader next time she came. "We're not even sure which of the big cobs is Bud and which is Carl, so hopefully Jane can check them too. I expect she can tell us which microchip company holds their details. We should register them all as being here."

A little while later Carrie went out to the back field and caught Monkey, with a head collar that was so big she could hardly keep it on him. She decided he'd had enough grass and was going to bring him into the stables for a few hours. All was well getting him out of the field, but as soon as he realised he was being taken away from his friends, and the free buffet, he dug in his heels and refused to move. Despite being small, there was no way Carrie could pull him along, so she sat down and waited for him to get bored. He was standing in the middle of the drive with no grass in reach. Carrie was holding him loosely, but ready to stop him going any way but the way she wanted. After a few minutes, Monkey started to fidget and snuffle around. This time when she stood and asked him to walk forward he took a few steps, then suddenly put on the brakes and refused to move again. Carrie sat down. "We can do this all day, my love, I've nowhere I have to be." After a few minutes Monkey started to fidget and snuffle again so Carrie asked him to walk on. They did this five times before Monkey finally gave in and walked happily beside her into the courtyard, and into the stables. She praised him and gave him a carrot she had in her pocket. He soon settled, with a small pile of hay and plenty of water he was content. Caleb appeared, looking over the door, as Carrie sat in the stable watching Monkey eat.

"You were a long time, I was just coming to find you when you appeared round the corner. Are you both OK?"

Carrie explained the battle of wills that she and Monkey had just had. Caleb was highly amused that something so small could cause such trouble. He said, "I think he's a permanent fixture here, don't you? I would love to see the others get good new homes one day, but Monkey needs to stay, he has such character, I love him already." Carrie willingly agreed. "I'm glad he's got to you too, he's ace, but you can lead him in and out every day! I don't think we've seen the last of his attitude yet, he'll be high maintenance I think."

Much later, as the sun was going down, Caleb went out to take Monkey back to the paddock and his friends. All went smoothly until they turned the corner, round the side of the courtyard, then Monkey took control once more.

Carrie looked up as she walked back from the cliff field, some movement caught her eye. As she focussed, she saw Monkey, his little legs moving like pistons, galloping towards the paddock. Caleb was still holding on, just, but was being dragged along so fast he could hardly keep upright, his legs were almost a blur. Just as she thought Caleb would surely fall over, the little pony reached the gate and stopped sharply. Caleb passed the pony and cannoned into the gate before he could stop himself. Carrie watched in horror as it happened, but as soon as she saw Caleb was in one piece, she cried with laughter. Monkey was grazing on the lush grass outside the field gate by the time she looked again, as if nothing had happened and butter wouldn't melt! Caleb was bent double and trying to catch his breath. She raced up the drive, reaching Caleb just as he stood upright again. With tears of laughter still streaming from her eyes, she hugged Caleb and took the lead rope from him. She put Monkey back in the field with his friends and wiped her eyes before Caleb saw. He was leaning on the gate, nursing his pride and some bruises, she imagined. As he caught her eye, she tried to look sympathetic. "Are you OK my love? That was some sprint!"

Caleb used a couple of very descriptive phrases, in relation to Monkey's parentage and future, as he got his composure back. She thought she heard him mention dog food and abattoirs under his breath too. Carrie tried to remain sympathetic, but she could feel the laughter bubbling up inside her. At that moment Caleb caught her eye again, within seconds they were both helpless with snorts of laughter, holding each other up as they gasped and howled. Carrie eventually got enough breath to speak, "Are you sure you're OK, you looked like you could beat Usain Bolt for a bit there." She fell about laughing again just as Caleb was recovering, he lost it again and they sat down hard on the verge with tears streaming and snot bubbles threatening. "I think I need oxygen," croaked Caleb, as he bent double again. Eventually, they both pulled themselves back into adulthood and their breathing returned to normal. Carrie joked, "I think we need a new gate, this one has a Caleb shaped dent in it now. Which bit hurts most?"

Caleb had a feel around his chest and shoulder. "I think I got away with just denting my pride, and the gate, of course. You can inspect me later for bruises." he winked. They headed back to the house giggling and discussing ways of curbing Monkey's behaviour.

Chapter 7

Recruiting

After another relaxing day, alone on their farm, with just the horses and the cat to interrupt their love making, Carrie didn't know whether to be happy or sad when Monday came. She had spent many happy hours checking Caleb for bruises, and the bed had definitely had its test drive, they even slept in it finally. She had loved the peace and intimacy of being alone with Caleb, but she was so excited to get started working on the farm and their future. Taking on their first staff member was a big step in making it all happen.

Mr Quaggan arrived at 8am promptly and came into the kitchen after knocking. "Mornin' Mr Kirk-michael, Mrs Jones. Bill from the building supplies place promised to have your delivery here by 11.30 this morning, hope that's OK with you?"

"That's wonderful," said Caleb, "and please use

our first names, I'm Caleb and this is Carrie. We can sit here and chat about your pay and stuff, before the supplies arrive, get everything agreed, so my accountant and lawyer can do you a contract. Carrie is an equal partner in all we do here, so you will be working for both of us. I'll put the kettle on and we'll discuss the rest."

If Mr Quaggan, or Juan, as he said to call him, was surprised that international film star Caleb made him tea, he hid it well. They chatted casually while the tea brewed. "Quaggan is an uncommon name Juan, is it Irish?" asked Carrie.

"No Mrs....Carrie, my family are from the Isle of Man, and the wife's. That's where we went for our holiday just now. We visited with family we hadn't seen for years and enjoyed the Manx fresh air and scenery. Have you ever been there?"

Caleb asked, "Is that the island just off the south coast here, I think I went as a child?"

Juan laughed. "No, that's the Isle of Wight, the Isle of Man is in the Irish Sea, sort of between Liverpool and Northern Ireland. Everyone gets them confused though. The Isle of Man has its own government and is steeped in Celtic history. I can't see us moving back there now, the kids are all here, but I still miss it. It was good to visit. I wondered if Caleb had Manx connections? Kirk Michael is a village on the Island."

Caleb laughed, "My real name is Caleb Michael, the Kirk bit got added when I first started acting, apparently it sounds classier, so my agent at the time thought anyway. I legally adopted the name as I got more famous. Maybe that agent had been to the Isle of Man on his holidays too?"

"What made you move over here?" Asked Carrie.

"Usual story, not much work on the Island, better pay over here – and we were young and looking for adventure. I like it well enough here now, and the wife loves being near the grand-kids."

"Can I ask how many years you have left before retirement Juan? If you turn out to be invaluable to us, as I think you will, I'd like to know how long I have to learn from you before you leave us." Caleb was planning ahead.

"I have six years left officially, but I can't imagine retiring, I like to be busy, so I won't be disappearing, unless I need to for my health or anything. I'm pretty fit and strong for an old fella!"

"Good news for us then Juan, thanks. Now about wages. I know we agreed to match your old wage but I think we can do better than that. I really need you to take control of all the land maintenance on the farm, as well as turn your hand to anything else we need. We can get in other staff as needed, but you know the land and your skills and experience will be key. I think I would call it a farm manager position really, but I need you to be hands on, not manage from an office. I have so much to learn and I'll need you to advise and teach me. I'll take responsibility for all decisions but I need your expertise to help me make those decisions. I don't want you to feel responsible, I like being responsible, but I do need your guidance as well as your graft, if you see what I mean? Does that sound OK with you? If so, then this is what we would pay you per month," he handed Juan a slip of paper with a figure on. Caleb and Carrie had agreed the amount earlier.

Juan stared and said, "You could get a younger, fitter man than me with that amount, it's much more than I'm worth, at my age."

Caleb laughed, "We think it's exactly what you're worth to us. A younger man would want to spray everything in sight with chemicals and grub out hedges to maximise profit. If I'm honest, we don't need or expect a profit, we need grassland and buildings for rescued horses, and I can afford to pay what it takes to get that, I'm very lucky. We want the farm kept the way it is now, you know how to keep it that way. That's priceless to us."

Carrie continued, "We're offering you 6 weeks holiday a year and we are open to negotiation if you need more as time goes on. We fully expect that you'll want to do less as the years pass, so we'll always listen if you need to discuss taking on an assistant or cutting your hours. It's not in our interests to wear you out! As long as you're flexible and happy to turn your hand to whatever we need, with help when necessary, we'll be happy. We thought 8am to 4.30pm Monday to Friday would be suitable hours for us, if you have different ideas then just say. We both like to finish what we start, so some overtime, to complete jobs, might be needed, paid at time and a half. Does that sound reasonable?"

Juan looked from one to the other of them suspiciously. "It all sounds too good to be true, what's the catch? - Sorry if that sounds ungrateful but you're offering me far more than the job is worth. I'm old, but not stupid, no one gives something for nothing these days."

Caleb looked taken aback, so Carrie answered quickly. "We need your knowledge of the land and we want you to stay, and be happy. Agricultural wages are really low, I worked in a stable yard, so I know how hard it is to survive on a low income. We don't want our workers to struggle, we want them to be happy here." Juan was still looking dubious. "I'll tell you what, why don't you start by working on those terms for a couple of months, call it a trial period. After two months we'll sit here again and you can tell us if you want to stay, and we can tell you the same. By then you'll know if there's a catch, or if we're just stupid rich people, paying over the odds for staff."

Juan suddenly looked embarrassed. "I'm sorry, I've been rude to you and you've been nothing but generous to me. I'm not used to this sort of luck and it's thrown me. I would love to take the job, on any terms. Two months trial will set my mind at rest that I can live up to your expectations. If you still want me then let's get started, I have a wage to earn."

Carrie smiled and Caleb said, "Good chap, I do understand your scepticism, but we are genuine people, I hope you'll come to realise that. I'll get the details all typed up and we'll both have a copy so we know where we stand. OK, let's go out and plan how we can make this fence work in the courtyard."

By the time the lorry with the fencing materials arrived, Caleb and Juan seemed to be getting along well. The slight disagreement over pay was forgotten and Juan had explained his fence plan to Caleb. Carrie had checked all the horses and put the cream on the two cobs backs. The rain scald, which is a sore and scabby skin condition, was definitely looking better, the skin looked less inflamed and some scabs were coming off. The weather was dry which was helping. She led Monkey in from the field to his stable, with only a couple of stops on the way. A pocket full of treats, for when he walked properly, was definitely helping. Carrie had plans to make Monkey his own little stable, with a lower door, in one of the courtyard pens. Then even when he was shut in, he would be able to watch them over the door. In the bigger stables he couldn't see over the door or out of the window at all, being so short. Carrie got Monkey settled in the stable just as the lorry drove in.

The driver and Caleb quickly unloaded the fence posts, wire, a gate and some wooden rails. He also brought some brackets, designed to be bolted into the concrete and hold the posts up. Juan had seen how small Monkey was as Carrie led him in, and laughed when Caleb worried the posts wouldn't be strong enough. Carrie smiled, remembering just how strong the little pony could be. She told Juan that she wanted it to be strong enough to hold bigger horses too. He assured her, with the long anchor bolts he had bought, the fence would hold a rhino. He said he helped to lay the concrete some years ago and knew it was strong and thick.

As the men got started with a noisy hammer drill on the concrete, Carrie checked Monkey wasn't scared of the noise. He was still happily munching on his hay and seemed oblivious. She left him to it and wandered around the courtyard, deciding which pen would be best for his new stable. Beside the house was a long open shed, probably designed to keep carts in originally. It was empty at present and had gates fitted across the front. She decided this was way too big for Monkey and not very cosy. Along the back of the yard, there were five smaller pens with stable type doors on. These looked like they had been used for pigs or calves, they were dirty and some obviously let the rain in. She looked in each and chose the best one, with no sign of leaks. This could be Monkey's stable. She spoke to Caleb and Juan and told them what she'd like to do. "I'm very happy to scrub it out and paint the walls, but could you two make a lower door to fit it, so Monkey can see over it?" Juan thought he could knock something up and Caleb suggested they make that their next job, when they had finished the fence. Carrie got to work scrubbing the pen out and disinfecting it.

By the early evening, when it was time to return Monkey to his field, Juan and Caleb had constructed a good strong fence across the yard. They'd used stock wire, with rails at the top for strength, it looked good. Juan set off for home and Caleb came to help take Monkey back out. They had found the smallest head collar that the farm shop had in stock but it was still a bit big. Carrie showed Caleb how to wrap the lead rope around Monkey's nose and tuck it through the head collar, it would tighten against his nose if he pulled hard and loosen if he stopped pulling. With this in place, they set off. Monkey must have realised he was not going to win this round, he walked along beside them as good as gold, all the way to the gate. They checked the others were all OK and returned to the house. Caleb made them a drink whilst Carrie admired the new fence.

The next morning Carrie's phone rang, just as she was putting cream on Bud and Carl's backs. Swearing about the timing, she wiped the cream off her hands down her legs and answered. "Carrie, it's Don, can I come for a chat? I was doing so well, but now I've hit rock bottom again. I'm frightened to be alone, frightened I'll just wallow in grief. I'm trying to stop brooding, like you said, but today's a bad day, it was our anniversary."

"Oh Don, of course you can, and stay as long as you want. We'll find stuff to do to keep you occupied, and as much time to chat as you need. Come now, I'll have the kettle on."

Carrie headed for the house to tell Caleb that Don was coming. She found him and Juan hanging a sweet little door on Monkey's new stable. "We found an old door round the back, which was in pretty good nick, so we cut it down and sanded the edges. We can use the old hinges, but I wasn't keen to cut down the original door, in case we want to put it back on later. What do you think?"

Carrie thought it was a great solution and thanked

them on Monkey's behalf. Monkey was currently wandering around his new pen, examining Juan's tool bag and generally getting in the men's way. Apparently, he had been in his stable a couple of times for a look and seemed to approve. He had hay and water near the fence, but he obviously thought bugging the men might get him something tastier. Carrie quietly told Caleb she'd be busy with Don for a while, he was pleased Don had asked for help but didn't say much in front of Juan.

Carrie went inside, put the kettle on and found four mugs, no need to ask who wanted one, she knew they all would. Don appeared a few minutes later, greeting Caleb and Juan as he came into the yard. He had a smile plastered on but Carrie could see the tension in his eyes. She finished making the tea, handed it out, and sat down in the kitchen with Don. "So, you had a couple of good days, that's wonderful. Have you found some new hobbies to keep you busy or have you been working?"

"When I left here on Friday, I felt so good. You and Caleb were amazing and Jane treated me like I was a normal person too. She seemed keen to chat, just about general stuff. It was so nice to feel like someone was seeing me, and not the grief. She's a lovely girl, shame about her shit of a boss, she deserves better."

"Oh, what's going on with her boss?"

"Well, it's common gossip so I'm sure I can tell you, apparently she and he were a couple for a while, then he met someone else and cheated on her. She confronted him at work and called him out in front of a couple of other staff because she was heart-broken. Now he treats her like the lowest of the low and makes her life hell. She's been looking for another job, but she has to stay around here, to look after her elderly mother. None of the other local practices are looking for vets at the minute. It's not fair, she was the victim of his infidelity, yet she's the one who's being punished. She's such a sweet person, and a good vet, she doesn't deserve this."

"Oh, that's awful for her, poor girl, she seems so nice. What a horrible trap to be in. The boss should be the one suffering, not her." Carrie was glad that Don was thinking and talking about someone else, forgetting his own problems for a while.

"Can't Jane set up her own practice or something, get away from the git and take a few clients with her to annoy him?"

"I asked her that on Friday, she doesn't feel she can afford to. Also, she's worried she won't be able to look after her mother if she's so busy building up a new practice. She seems trapped for now."

"Hmm, I wonder if we can help? We were planning to have an in-house vet here eventually. Maybe we should talk to her, see if the promise of that, in a few months time, might give her a light at the end of the tunnel. I'll talk to Caleb and see what we can come up with."

"Carrie, you and Caleb should get a knighthood! You've been here five minutes and you are already rescuing all the waifs and strays, human as well as animal! Is there anyone you won't rescue?" Don was smiling a genuine smile now.

"Hey, I was one of those waifs and strays not long ago, I'm just passing on the help my friends gave me. Having Caleb's millions to do it with, is a powerful and exciting experience. Don't tell anyone I said that though, I am trying to convince the world that his money is nothing to do with why I love him," she giggled.

Don laughed. "Anyone can see you are totally smitten, if Caleb was a homeless bum, you'd still love him – it shines from you when he is around."

"Thanks, Don, that's exactly how I feel, nice to see it shows. I'd hate to be thought of as a money grabber."

"People always jump to conclusions, don't they? You're a money grabber, I'm a grieving time bomb, ready to explode and make them uncomfortable. Why can't people just accept who we are? God Carrie, I miss her so much, she always accepted me for me, never made me feel inadequate or lacking. She was my confidence and now that's gone." The tears came and Don looked away.

"Don, you don't have to hide your tears here, remember? This is your place for accepting that tears are a part of the current you. I've shed so many, they don't make you weak, or unmanly, or childlike or any of those things. They just are, they're not who you are."

"Oh Carrie, we grow up believing men don't cry, crying is for babies, all that stuff. I feel so useless when I cry. I never cried before Laura died, not since

I was a kid, I had no need to, I was whole. She was here." Don wept for a few minutes. Carrie sat and waited.

"How long has it been since she died, tell me about it, about her," Carrie said quietly as Don dried his eyes.

"Carrie she was lovely, like you in a way, kind and wise. She didn't look like you though, she was blond and tall and beautiful, to me anyway. She died suddenly, of an undiscovered cancer. One week she was feeling a bit rough, the next week she was in agony and the next she was gone, it was like my worst nightmare. It was eighteen months ago, and today would have been our fifteenth anniversary."

"Did you have children?"

"No, she couldn't, but it never worried me, we were a team, us against the world. She encouraged me to be the best I could be, take extra training courses, expand my farrier skills. I would be working on a building site, as a labourer or something, without her to make me see my abilities. She believed in me, and I don't know how to believe in myself without her."

"I believe in you, your work with our horses was as good as anyone I've seen before. I'm no expert, but the horses were all uncomfortable before you came and comfortable when you left. You did that. I think you have to train yourself to believe in you now. She gave you a great gift by believing in you. You need to value that gift, by carrying on the belief yourself. Don't let what she gave you go to waste. Make it a gift to her memory, to believe in yourself like she believed in you. Achieve for her. One day you will realise she was right to believe in you, you are good."

"Do you charge by the hour for this?" Don smiled. "You seem to know what I am feeling, when I don't, and what buttons to press to make me feel strength again. I can believe in myself for Laura, even if I can't do it for myself. That makes perfect sense to me. Thanks Carrie."

"You will get highs and lows, that's normal too, just go with it. I still get moments, but rarely lately. I held on to the pain too long, don't make that mistake. Open yourself to new possibilities, don't feel guilty for feeling good when it happens. Anyone who loved you would want you to have a happy future."

Carrie added, "On a different subject for a

moment, I need to walk up to the cliff field and check the horses up there, will you walk with me? We can chat as we go."

"Sounds good to me, I've no jobs to do today, so if I can help with anything, just say. It'll do me good to be busy. I saw Monkey in the yard, I'll have a quick look at his feet in a bit, not that they will have changed much in four days, but he's good company too!"

They set off towards the cliff field, waving to Juan and Caleb as they went. Carrie had no idea what they were doing, it looked like they were discussing the implements in the machinery barn. She was so glad Caleb and Juan were working well together. Juan seemed happy to have Caleb as an apprentice, and Caleb was full of praise for Juan's knowledge and teaching skills.

As they walked Carrie decided to broach the subject of Jane again. "Don, I noticed you and Jane were enjoying chatting, why don't you pursue the friendship? Both of you could do with a close friend right now. You could help her to feel better about her work situation, give her a boost when she's down."

"I don't think I'm any use to anyone at the minute. I'm not ready to date, if that's what you mean?"

"No, I don't mean dating, I mean just someone to go out with as a friend. So you can get used to being in the world again. So she can enjoy getting out with someone who appreciates her, she must be feeling a bit like a castoff at present."

"I don't know if I can do it though. What if she doesn't want a friend? What if I cry?"

"How about if we have a 'thank you' party here for you both, just something informal and relaxed? You could see if anything came of spending time with her, without any pressure, in a friendly gathering."

"That couldn't do any harm I guess, she won't think I am chasing her or anything. Would you do that? It seems to put you to a lot of bother, and you are paying for our services, you don't have to thank us."

"You need to believe in yourself remember, you and Jane both went above and beyond what you are billing us for on Friday, you both deserve thanks."

"You haven't seen the bill yet!" laughed Don.

As they reached the field gate Carrie stopped. She could see one of the bigger horses lying down, there was nothing strange about that, but something didn't look quite right about him. Don saw it too, they both rushed over, slowing as they neared him, so as not to upset him. It was Sonny, and the poor horse was breathing really hard and sweating. Carrie felt his pulse and it was fast but not strong. She remembered Jane said he had a slight heart murmur, and her heart sank.

Don was already on his phone, "Hi Jane it's Don, I'm at Cliff Top Farm and one of the horses is seriously ill, can you come asap, or should I ring the practice?"

Carrie didn't hear Jane's answer, she found her own phone and called Caleb. Within a minute, she heard the car roaring up the track from the yard.

Don said. "We just caught Jane going for her lunch, she is on her way now, I told her this was the one with the heart murmur, was I right?" Carrie nodded.

Caleb and Juan were now running over the field towards them. "Is he OK, will he make it," asked Caleb looking pale.

"I don't know, but it doesn't look good, I think it's his heart," Carrie said.

She looked around the field in case there was any other possible causes, poisonous plants or something that could have caused his collapse. Everything looked fine, including the other three horses, who were watching from a short distance away. She asked Caleb to go and check them, whilst she knelt beside Sonny. She stroked his neck and whispered soothing words, but she didn't think he was aware of her, he was fighting for his life with every breath.

Within minutes they heard Jane's car approaching. Juan went back to the gate and waved so she came to the right field. She drove straight in and over to Sonny. Jane listened to his heart and breathing then stood up. "I'm really sorry but his heart is failing, it's most likely that the heart murmur got worse. He needs to be put to sleep to ease his suffering, he's not going to recover and he must feel awful."

Carrie nodded. "Do it. He doesn't need to suffer

anymore."

Caleb asked, "Are you sure there's no hope? We can try anything, I'll pay whatever it takes."

Jane shook her head. "I'm as sure as I can be that he's dying, and we can make it quick, rather than leaving him like this. Can I go ahead?"

Caleb nodded. Carrie went to him and gave him a hug, then went back to Sonny and stroked his neck, as the drugs to end his life were injected. The drugs worked really quickly and his breathing slowed and stopped. Jane listened with her stethoscope and nodded sadly. Carrie leant down and whispered goodbye in his ear and gave him a kiss. When she returned to Caleb's arms, she was crying hard.

Chapter 8

Toughening

Caleb held Carrie tight as they looked down at poor Sonny. Jane and Don stood side by side and Don was wiping a tear. Jane noticed and handed him a tissue, without a word. She squeezed his arm and moved away to pack up her stuff. Juan stood a little way off, looking uncomfortable.

Jane explained what she thought had happened. "When I diagnosed the heart murmur, I knew this was a possibility. Mostly, if the murmur is caused purely by lack of nutrition, the heart recovers as nutrition improves, but occasionally, the damage is too great. It's possible there was previous heart damage, or there was some other underlying weakness. I was very hopeful that all would be well, but there are no guarantees. I'm really sorry, but there was nothing you, or anyone else, could have done, it was just his time to go. I can arrange a post mortem if you like but it's unlikely that it will tell us much more than we know already. You made his last few days happy and comfortable, much better than dying hungry and dirty in that other place."

Caleb reached out for Jane and gave her a hug, "Thanks for coming so quickly and being so sympathetic. I realise I'm probably the only one here who has never seen a horse, or any other animal, dying like that, it really shook me. Thank you for taking charge and telling me it was time. Thank you for stopping Sonny from suffering anymore."

Carrie smiled at him and said. "I've seen it before, more than once, so it was a bit easier for me, I could see it was time. Thank you all for rushing to his aid, I feel glad he had these few days here, as Jane says, he was happy, with a belly full of grass at the end."

Juan coughed, "Can I go down to the house and make us all a cup of tea? I can call the knacker man too if you like?"

Carrie smiled, "Yes please to the tea, I'm not sure about the knacker man, we need to discuss this, it's not something we expected to have to deal with yet, but tea is always a good idea."

Juan headed off back to the house. Carrie invited Don and Jane to join them and they all headed back, either on foot or in cars. Caleb seemed confused and asked, "who's the knacker man, or don't I want to know?" Don and Carrie smiled.

"Have you ever thought about what you do with the body of a dead horse?" asked Don.

"Oh God, I am now!" Caleb said ruefully.

"We have two options I think," said Carrie, "either we look up the regulations for burying him here, on the farm, or we call the knacker man."

"Do I want to know where the knacker man takes him?" asked Caleb.

"Probably not," said Carrie and Don in unison.

They reached the house just as the tea was brewed. Jane and Juan were chatting at the kitchen table. Carrie found some biscuits for everyone and joined the others. "Sonny can stay where he is for a while. The other horses will go for a look and a smell. Sometimes they seem more settled when they can do that, rather than when the horse is taken straight away. I'm never sure if that's wishful thinking on our part, or if they really understand death." said Carrie.

Jane replied, "I don't think anyone has proved or disproved it scientifically, it's possible they have some level of understanding. It always amazes me how much they are aware of. They were definitely standing guard near Sonny when we were with him. I wonder if they knew he was ill? They would usually stand near if one of them was lying down anyway, so it's hard to tell. They usually look after each other when they rest, there's nearly always one standing up and keeping watch, while the others are lying down or dozing. It's a fascinating subject."

"So, are we going to try and bury him on the farm?" asked Caleb.

"We should look into it, but, when we are fully up and running, are you going to want every dead animal buried here? There will be many more over time. I think you have to bury them with loads of lime, be careful with watercourses and the way the land drains and things. You probably have to get a licence too. It may be better to call the knacker man in the end, Sonny won't know, so it's only our own feelings we are trying to save. We can do a bit of research online before we decide."

"I'm amazed how matter of fact you are about it Carrie, I'm glad you are calm and I'm the one who is finding this so hard," said Caleb.

"I've been here before, it's an unpleasant part of the responsibility of keeping animals. I've just got a bit more used to it than you I guess. Losing an animal never gets easier but dealing with the practicalities does."

"What would the rest of you do?" Caleb asked the others.

Don and Juan agreed with Carrie, that the knacker man was the usual solution for farmers and most other people. Jane said, "There are crematoriums that can deal with bigger animals but that would be prohibitively expensive for most people. You need to think if going to that expense is really the best use of your money. It's not going to help the horse, he's gone. It is only our human squeamishness that we are satisfying with burials or cremation. The best way, logically, is for the animal's body to be reused in some way, which is where the knacker man came in, traditionally."

"I hate logic at times," Caleb said, "but thanks for the answers, I think."

Carrie gave him a big hug. "No one said it would be easy, and it will be worth the heartache when the others recover and get new homes. Concentrate on that bit."

"I guess I should call Babs and let her know, why do I feel that we have failed in some way?"

Jane said, "It would have made no difference if Sonny had stayed with that sanctuary or come here, he would still be gone. Nothing could have been done to change it, either by them or by you. Stop beating yourself up, you gave these horses the best chance of recovery."

"Thanks Jane, that helps, I knew death would be part of helping animals, but knowing and actually experiencing are different things, I guess. You think you are realistic and logical about it until it actually happens, then the emotions kick in. I will toughen up eventually."

"I kind of like soft Caleb, don't get too hardened my sweet," Carrie said, getting up and kissing the top of his head. "Anyone want more tea?"

"No thanks, I must get to my next call," said Jane standing to leave. "Oh, I nearly forgot, I got the last of the blood test results and there is nothing to report, they are all good."

"Thanks, that's good news. Something I forgot to ask you too, my horse is supposed to be arriving tomorrow, is it safe for him to mix with the others do you think, they don't seem to be carrying anything contagious?"

"I'm pretty sure they are fine, but to be totally sure I would just put him in a field away from the rest for a few weeks and maybe wash between handling the others and handling him to be really safe. Over time, if you are rescuing others, he will be exposed to risk at some point. Set yourself up a quarantine area for any new admissions, that way all the others will be safer. Oh, and make sure you keep his inoculations up to date of course."

"Thanks Jane, see you soon."

"Bye everyone." Jane headed off to her next case.

"I hope she gets time for something to eat, she needs to look after herself," worried Don.

Carrie and Caleb shared a secret smile.

Chapter 9

Planning

When everyone else had left, Carrie and Caleb lay on the sofa discussing the day's events. Caleb had rung Babs with their sad news. As expected, Babs was practical and understanding about it. They discussed what to do with Sonny's body. Caleb came around to the idea of the knacker man when Babs explained that, in both their areas, the council disposed of all waste, including large animals, in a huge incinerator that generates electricity. The knacker man was actually a council employee, who collected livestock bodies around the farms. Bodies were no longer sold to dog meat factories or glue makers! Caleb felt he could cope with Sonny going that way and Carrie was relieved it was sorted. She called and arranged the collection for the following morning.

Babs also had some other exciting news. The only remaining relative of the old lady, who owned all the rescued horses, had been traced. The relative had legally signed all the horses over to the sanctuary, as she did not have any wish to keep them. So the horses were all the property of the sanctuary and no one could make a claim for them. They were safe.

The last bit of news Babs had was good, but got them both thinking hard. The two piebald cobs, Bud and Carl, might have a new, forever home. Babs explained, she'd had a call from Pat, a lady she had known for years. Pat knew the old owner and had tried to buy Bud and Carl from her a number of times over the years. The old lady wouldn't part with them. Pat ran a business hiring horse-drawn vehicles for weddings and events. The two cobs would be perfect for her business. Finding a well matched pair of horses to pull a cart was always difficult. Babs knew Pat was a genuine and committed horse owner and that Bud and Carl would be very well looked after. Babs suggested letting Pat have the two cobs now, as she had the experience to get them fit and well. Babs would keep an eye on them there, she just wondered how Caleb and Carrie would feel about them going so soon. Caleb had told her he liked the idea but needed to talk to Carrie before agreeing to it.

Carrie had been thinking for a while about the

new home for the cobs. She finally said, "This home with Pat sounds too good to miss, Carl and Bud will thrive having a job to do. It sounds like Babs knows they'll be well looked after. Lucky Pat, getting them for free, having wanted to buy them for years. I hope she offers Babs a good donation for the sanctuary. I'll be sad to see them go, but this is what we wanted, good lives for any animal we can re-home, we should agree to it. Maybe we can ask that they stay here a couple more weeks to get stronger first. Another journey so soon would be hard on them. If this Pat has their welfare at heart, I'm sure she'll agree."

Caleb nodded, "That sounds like a good plan. I'll call Babs in the morning and see if she agrees. Our first re-homed animals, our first death, and our first staff member, it's been some week, and it's only Tuesday!"

"Sally, Terry and Bilbo are coming tomorrow lunchtime, I can't wait! I need to choose a field for him, the one I chose before is already full of ponies. I think I'll use one of the ones near the barn, then I can shut him in a pen for a while each day. The field we landed the helicopter in, on our first visit, will be good, apart from the lush grass, we'll just have to limit his time on it. He should be able to see the other horses from there too, so he won't feel so lonely. I just need to check the fences and double check all the rusty bits of metal got removed, do you remember how many old farm implements were sat there when we first arrived? I'll disinfect a pen for him too, just to be safe, as the others have been in the barn."

Caleb laughed. "I remember the rusty bits well, they sold the farm to us, before we even got out of the chopper! Juan and I can check the field and clean out the trough for Bilbo. You concentrate on getting a pen ready. Maybe we could put up a temporary fence to limit him to a small part of the field? That way he could stay out all day. I'll ask Juan's advice, he has a solution for most things. Once Bilbo's here, I think I should do all the checking of the rescue horses and bring Monkey in each day. That way you only need to handle Bilbo and you won't have to worry about carrying germs to him."

"That would make me feel happier, thanks sweetie. It'll only be for a few weeks. We should make building a quarantine area a priority, so we don't have worries in the future."

They chatted about the quarantine area for a while, choosing a site and thinking about what they needed to build. Once they had a picture in their head, they moved on to talk about the house renovations. They would plan it with a contractor, tell him what they wanted and let the contractor do the lot. Carrie was used to having to do things like decorating herself, she offered to do it, but Caleb wouldn't hear of it. He would rent them a house locally, so they could move out for the months it would take. Carrie wasn't too sorry that they weren't doing it themselves, as long as the finished project was how they wanted it. Sometimes it was nice to let Caleb take control and be masterful! All she said was, "Can we wait until after the winter? With all these horses here there's loads of work to do, it'll be easier to be living here for that. We can get stuck into the outside renovations and building over the winter maybe?"

They lay there, planning, until late in the evening. It felt like they were really getting a picture of how it would all grow now. Eventually, Caleb said, "There are two more things we haven't discussed yet. The first one is a house warming party. It'll be great to have an outdoor, muddy get together for all our friends. We can use a barn, just in case the weather's bad and everyone can sit on straw bales, in their old clothes, and eat and drink. Some of my friends will come all dolled up but that's their problem. We can just be in jeans and wellies and be happy. What do you think?"

"Sounds perfect, we could invite some locals, get to know a few more people too? And Babs."

Great, let's make it a bonfire party, it'll soon be cold, no fireworks of course, but a big fire and maybe a band or something. What about mid-November?

"Sounds good, what's the other thing?"

Caleb kissed her neck and whispered, "I want you to be Mrs Kirkmichael soon."

Carrie smiled, she knew she was ready for that one. "OK."

"Just OK?"

"Well, it would be nice to have a summer wedding, outside, here, with horses and dogs and fields and friends, hog roasts and barbecues and no girlie white dresses or penguin suits. But I'm open to suggestions. Not that I've thought about it at all, ever!!"

They both laughed, "I think we're a perfect match, the sooner I make you my wife the better."

Chapter 10

Reuniting

It was nearly two o'clock and Carrie was bursting with excitement. Not only was her precious Bilbo arriving soon, but her bestie Sally was bringing him, and they could chat all afternoon. Of course it was raining, but nothing could dampen her enthusiasm today. Caleb was also looking forward to seeing Sally again and meeting her husband Terry.

They'd spent the morning getting Bilbo's field and pen ready. Juan had gone off to the farm supplies shop to buy some electric fence equipment, so they could restrict Bilbo to a smaller part of the field. He had explained to Caleb how it worked and Carrie, who hadn't even thought of this solution, was over the moon with his idea. She wouldn't have to shut Bilbo up in a pen, he could have a small patch of grass, and wander in and out of the pen as he chose. When he had eaten that patch of grass he could be given a little more, just by moving the fence a bit. If he tried to push through the fence, the small electric current would give him a tiny, harmless but unpleasant shock, which would make him avoid it in future. A safe and portable solution that she could adapt to use with Monkey as well.

Just after 2pm she heard a rumble as Sally's lorry came up the drive. They went out to greet them and show them to the barn. Sally and Terry waved as they drove up and Sally jumped down as soon as she stopped the lorry. Carrie hugged her forever and when Terry appeared, he got a hug too. Carrie opened the groom's door of the lorry to greet Bilbo. He looked handsome and happy standing and pulling hay out of his hay-net. She rubbed his forehead and said hello. He snuffled her hand for a treat and she imagined he was pleased to see her, as it made her feel good. Terry and Caleb lowered the ramp at the back of the lorry and Carrie led Bilbo down and into his pen. They all stood leaning on the rails of the pen and watched as Bilbo explored his new home. He soon found the pile of hay Carrie had left for him and tucked in happily. They could give him a section of the field to graze later on, once the electric fence arrived.

After a quick look around the barns, they all

headed back to the house for a cuppa and a chat. Carrie had been to the village shop that morning and bought cream cakes, they had a calorie filled half-hour whilst they caught up on each other's news. Sally sighed, "It's so peaceful here, all I can hear is birdsong and no traffic noise. When can we move in Terry?"

Terry laughed. "If you think I'm packing up all our stuff and moving, you are sadly mistaken. I love our little yard in Elver, we're not going anywhere."

Sally said, "You're right, our home and yard are just perfect, I love the peace here though, Elver seems to get busier every year."

"So how are all the horses at yours Sally are they well? Do you have someone to fill Bilbo's place yet?" Carrie asked.

"Everyone is fine, and Bilbo's space could have been filled five times over, so we are considering adding a few more stables next year. Janine, the new assistant is really good, we're not close like you and I were, but she's very reliable and works hard. I'm so glad I advertised for a more mature person again, it gives me peace of mind. I still miss you like crazy though Carrie, are you sure you wouldn't like to give all this up and come back?"

Carrie laughed, "I'm afraid not, I'm living the dream!"

"Ooh, I saw Dave and Gregg at the weekend, in the Co-op. They seemed really happy. I told them I was coming to see you and they sent loads of love. They said to tell you they are still deciding where their future lies, and whether they are ready for a mortgage, so they hoped they could rent for another year while they think it over."

"Bless them, Gregg has to think everything through for ages. I'm sure Dave is desperate to be more settled, maybe get married, but Gregg's not quite there yet. They can stay as they are, in the house, as long as they want. I'll ring them for a chat soon."

Caleb and Terry were chatting away in the sitting room, Caleb was showing Terry the stuff he was planning to install in the house. The ground source heat pump he wanted was a new idea to Carrie, and Terry seemed very interested in it.

Carrie and Sally went for a look around the house, then headed to the courtyard to meet Monkey and see the stables. Terry and Caleb decided to join them for a trip around the yard, then around the farm. Carrie warned Sally about the horses being in quarantine, she said she would just wash and change before she handled her own horses. Monkey heard them coming out of the back door, and was by the new fence, whinnying at them as they appeared. Carrie had them in stitches when she described Caleb's impromptu sprint behind Monkey the other evening. Yet again, Monkey had a fan club, as Sally and Terry fell for his charms. "Awww, he's so sweet, can I re-home him?" Sally begged.

Carrie laughed. "Join the queue, he's on everyone's Christmas list, but we've decided to keep him here, so no one will get a look in."

"He's trouble, anyway, you couldn't handle him." laughed Caleb.

They looked at the stables and admired all the buildings of the courtyard. "It's such a pretty stone they're all built of, is it a local one?" asked Terry.

"I'm sure it is, there are quite a few old buildings

around that are built of the same stuff. I'll have to find out where it was quarried," Caleb answered.

"Let's go for a walk around the land as it's stopped raining. We can enjoy a view of the sea from the cliffs and you can see the other rescue horses as we go round."

They enjoyed a long, leisurely walk around the fields and over to the cliffs. "Can you get down to the beach to ride from here?" asked Sally. "I've always wanted to ride on a beach but never managed it."

"Sadly, the cliffs are too steep here, but there's a road that goes down to the beach just a mile or so away. I'm looking forward to riding down there soon, to see what it's like. Next time you come I'll make sure there's a horse you can ride and we'll go together," said Carrie.

"That's definitely a date, have you thought of finding a horse for Caleb yet? The big bay horse, Jaffa, looks his size, he reminds me of Nero a bit, and Caleb loved him."

"To be honest, we haven't had time to even think about it yet, but Jaffa seems to have a nice character.

Once he's put on a bit more weight, and his feet are good, I'll start riding him and see how he goes. Caleb, what do you think of keeping Jaffa for you to ride?"

Caleb was walking behind with Terry, he looked up and grinned. "Great idea, if he's good to ride, how soon can we try him?"

Carrie thought for a bit, then said, "We can start handling him more anytime, to get him used to us grooming him and things, it'll probably be a month or two before he's healthy enough to ride."

"I can wait for him to be ready. Maybe we could put him in the field with Bilbo when his quarantine ends. They can become friends and we can handle them both together."

They returned from their walk and spent the rest of the afternoon chatting in the kitchen. Carrie was so happy to catch up on news of all the horses at Sally's yard. Caleb and Terry enjoyed discussing plans for the farm. Juan arrived back from the farm shop with the electric fencing, so they spent half an hour setting up Bilbo's grazing area and letting him out. He was very happy munching on the grass by the time Sally

126

and Terry hugged them both goodbye and set off for home.

A couple of nights later, Carrie was cooking a big saucepan of chilli con carne and another of rice. Don and Jane were coming for their 'thank you' meal. Caleb had bought some wine and a very sticky looking caramel dessert, from the village shop. They both knew the chilli was the limit of Carries cooking skills and a dessert was best bought in! Caleb's cooking skills were not any better and neither of them had any inclination to improve. Caleb laid the table and found some plain yoghurt, which they loved with chilli. As he finished there was a knock, and Jane and Don let themselves in the back door. "Hi guys, pick a seat, I think it's nearly ready. Can I pour you both some wine?" Caleb became the perfect host, chatting away as he poured. Carrie loved watching him when he was like this, there were never any awkward silences and everyone felt relaxed. She stirred the chilli as she listened in to Caleb's conversation, smiling and suddenly feeling so content. This was the first time they had hosted a meal, she realised. They'd told Don and Jane not to dress up or anything, Carrie was glad to see they were both in jeans. Caleb carried the chilli to the table, still in the saucepan, and placed it on a trivet in the centre, Carrie brought the rice, drained and in a bowl, and some big serving ladles. "No ceremony tonight, just dig in and have as much as you want. I think I've made enough for a small army but I can freeze any we leave." Carrie placed a ladle in the rice and passed it to Don. He served Jane first, in a very gentlemanly way, and passed the bowl on to Caleb, who served himself and Carrie. They all took turns at ladling out the chilli and settled back to eat. Caleb carried on his conversation, by thanking them both for their recent help, and toasting his hope for many more times spent working together. Everyone raised a glass to that. Carrie added her thanks and asked if they had both had busy days. Don amused them with a story of a small pony that had nearly got the better of him that morning. It sounded like the pony did not enjoy his pedicure at all, and showed it by giving Don a good few bruises. Jane was watching him with a soft smile, Carrie noticed. Jane said she had a boring day doing paperwork, the thought of it made her look stressed, so Carrie quickly changed the subject. "I know you both live in the village, do you live close to each other?" she asked.

"We're quite close," said Don, "just a couple of minutes walk, I expect. We used to bump into each other in the pub every now and then, but I stopped going when........" Don faltered and a tear escaped. Caleb jumped in and started telling tales of the acting world to cover the silence. Carrie thought about giving Don a comforting hug, then she realised Jane had put her hand on his knee. Carrie was quietly overjoyed to have been beaten to it by Jane. The conversation carried on and Don seemed to recover his composure. Carrie secretly looked to see if Jane's hand was still on his knee later, but it wasn't. "Oh well, a good start," she said to herself smiling. They finished their chilli and had a few moments to digest before dessert.

Caleb offered everyone more wine. Don refused, as he was driving, but Jane accepted happily. "Don kindly offered to drive us both, so I'll make the most of it and have another, it would be rude not too!"

After dessert Carrie offered coffee and everyone accepted. They moved to the sitting room and chatted for an hour or so, putting the world to rights. Both Don and Jane were great company and they all seemed to be becoming good friends. Jane mentioned a local gig that she was going to and Don asked if she would like some company. She looked really happy as she accepted. Carrie caught Caleb's eye and he winked at her, smiling. As they left, at the end of the evening, Carrie gave them both a hug and thanked them for their company. Watching them drive off she hugged Caleb and said, "I think they are going to be fine, no more matchmaking needed there!" Caleb had to agree.

*   *   *   *   *

Over the next few weeks everything really started to change around the farm. Carrie was busy preparing for winter, deciding which horses needed to be stabled to protect them from the worst weather. They bought all of them cosy, waterproof rugs, so when they were outside, they had protection from the rain and wind. Even Monkey had a tiny little rug to wear, although he was growing such a thick hairy coat Carrie suspected he wouldn't need it. The risk of the new horses having any infections was minimal now, so all the horses were brought to fields nearer the house for the winter. Jaffa and Bilbo had become firm friends, living together in the 'helicopter' field and sharing access to a big pen in the barn if they wanted to shelter. Monkey was out with the three other smaller ponies full time, the grass was less nutritious now the weather was colder. All four had been moved to a bigger field with more grass. The two smaller cobs had access to shelter in the barn from their new field, which was next to Bilbo and Jaffa's. The two black and white cobs had gained lots of weight and were being picked up by their new owner very soon, they stayed where they were until then.

Carrie and Caleb had advice from Babs, when she visited, and had put in planning applications for two more huge barns in front to the original two. The long-term plan was to use one as a dedicated quarantine area, with its own big field at the side, for any new animals, large or small. The other would house a veterinary area and inside cages and pens for smaller animals to live in. Babs had told them there seemed to be huge numbers of dogs needing rescuing and re-homing that year, so they decided to fit out an area for housing dogs straight away. They had made a good case for the planners by saying how many local jobs they could create, once they were up and running, and they were hopeful that the planners would be kind.

Work on the courtyard buildings was already well underway. The builders were repairing the roofs and repointing the stone. Caleb was determined that there would be little change to the character of the courtyard and had insisted on using reclaimed materials to match the original. The five pens along the back were left alone apart from the roof being repaired, Carrie planned to use them as stables for the three small ponies as well as Monkey. The two-storey stable block and hay store was in good condition but needed a bit of repointing in places where damp was getting in. The glass in the big windows was replaced with special strong safety glass and they fitted shutters outside that could be closed for extra warmth. Bilbo, Jaffa and the two small cobs could be housed in there when the weather got really bad. Their initial plan, to keep the courtyard private, had been put on hold, as Carrie wanted all the horses within easy reach for the winter. As the big cobs were leaving soon, she didn't need to prepare for them. She planned to use the second storey of the stable building as a tack and rug store. It was fitted out with a few saddle racks and a big long bar to hang rugs over. She had room in the aisle downstairs to keep a few bales of hay and straw and the rest could stay in the barn. The courtyard work was scheduled to be finished within a fortnight and Carrie couldn't wait to get her horses in and settled.

Work on the two new barns couldn't really start yet, but planning the layout inside the barns had taken up many happy, evening hours and a few calls to Babs for advice. Babs' sanctuary had grown organically, as the money to expand had been raised. She was deeply jealous of them, planning from scratch and getting it right from the start, but very enthusiastic with her advice and help. Learning from her experiences was such a help to Carrie and Caleb. The quarantine barn needed pens for larger animals with access to the field, these would be along the far side of the barn, with solid dividing walls and small outside yards so the animals could have fresh air and a view, even if they could not go in the field. Inside it needed smaller pens for dogs and cats and an area for veterinary care that was separate from other treatment rooms. Once the animals were healthy and out of quarantine they could be in bigger pens in the other barn, or out in the fields. Further back in the barn, was a storage area for feed and equipment. Caleb and Babs had planned it so one or two staff could work in there and keep well away from the rest of the farm's animals. The vet may have to visit, but vets were used to being careful about spreading illness, so good practice and disinfectant should keep everyone safe. The quarantine field was double fenced by Juan so that any quarantined animals were kept from touching healthy animals. The gap left in between the fences could be used for exercising quarantined dogs when necessary, as dog diseases were not generally contracted by field animals and vice versa.

At about this time, Carrie and Caleb had some serious discussions about the staff they needed. Don was seeming stronger every week. He was still coming for his chats with Carrie, but increasingly, the chats were more relaxed and the crying had stopped. Caleb and Don had a long chat about the future, both of the farm, and for Don himself. Don had agreed to base his work at the farm, looking after Carrie and Caleb's horses as a priority. He would still work for his existing customers but also take a wage from the Sanctuary for part of the week. That way, he was not pressured to drum up new customers but he could still work for those who had stayed with him through his dark times.

Juan was really happy in his work and his trial period had been forgotten, he was staying. He was tending the fields lovingly, fixing anything that needed fixing and helping with planning the new areas. Caleb had bought a huge new muck hoover/ sweeper for the fields when he realised Carrie was trying to clean the fields by hand. Juan happily towed it around all the grazed fields, every morning, and kept them clean. They all wanted to minimise the use of chemical fertilizers and other sprays, so a big muck heap was started near the barns, in an old silage clamp. Once the muck had rotted for a couple of years it could be safely reapplied to the land as fertiliser. In the meantime, Juan had found a local farming friend who had cow muck they could have to fertilise with.

At the end of October, Juan suggested it was time to go round all the fields cutting back the hedges. He explained this was best done just before winter to keep them neat and stop them from growing out too far into the fields. Cutting them now, after all the birds had finished nesting but before the new growth of spring, meant the birds and the hedgerows stayed healthy. Caleb was keen to be involved, so they got the bigger tractor out for the first time. It had a small flip-down passenger seat, which Juan could sit in to instruct Caleb in the art of flailing a hedge. Caleb had got the hang of the smaller tractor fairly quickly but this one had many more levers and dials. Despite looking complex, he found the basic principals were the same. After half an hour of driving around the tracks they returned to the machinery barn and Juan showed him how to hitch up the flail mower. Once Caleb got the hang of moving the mower around on its long arm, they drove to the first field to start. Juan tried to sit calmly, as Caleb struggled with the coordination of driving the tractor slowly forward whilst watching the mower arm behind and making sure it cut the right bits off the hedge. By the time they reached the end of the field Juan looked pretty stressed, and so did the hedge! He asked if Caleb would like to watch while he cut the next length. They swapped places and Caleb watched intently as Juan cut a lovely neat swathe of hedge in one easy run. Caleb decided that Juan could do the rest. He would practice ready for next year.

Carrie and Caleb had discussed needing a vet for Cliff Top. They did not really need one full time for another year or so, but when Carrie explained Jane's predicament to Caleb it started him thinking. Jane was coming that morning to check on Cloud, who was not putting on weight as well as hoped. Caleb suggested they offer her a future at Cliff Top and see what she thought. If she still felt trapped and unhappy at the Scarton Practice, they could offer her general work as well as veterinary work until the sanctuary got going. When the work increased, she could work full time as a vet for them. Jane arrived just before lunch and they went to look at Cloud, who was in the barn having some extra feed. Carrie explained to Jane that, although Cloud was having the best grass and feed, he was still looking less well than the others. They knew he was quite old but wanted to check there was nothing else wrong. Jane gave him a good check over and looked at his teeth. She stood back and said, "He has a couple of sharp spurs on his teeth that may mean eating is a bit painful. Everything else looks OK, so that should be our first treatment. I can rasp the teeth down a bit, so they are not as sharp, but I would advise getting a proper equine dentist to check him, and all the others. Keeping their teeth in good shape can make a huge difference to their well-being." Jane headed to her car and fetched a rasp and a huge metal and leather contraption. Caleb took one look at it, and said, "What is that medieval looking torture device!" Jane and Carrie laughed. "It's just to keep his mouth open, so I can rasp his teeth. It looks worse than it is," Jane explained, as she slipped it over Cloud's head and placed the worst looking bit in his mouth. He didn't seem to mind too much and stood still while Carrie held him. Jane got to work. The rasp was as big as a woodworker's tool and Jane used it to smooth off the sharp edges of Cloud's teeth. She explained that horses' teeth don't have nerves like ours and they grow continuously through most of the horse's life. Cloud would only feel the strange sensation of the rasping, not any pain. She also said, from looking at his teeth, he was probably well over twenty years old. His teeth would have stopped growing at that age, so she only took off the bare minimum to get the teeth to sit smoothly together without any harsh edges. "An expert dentist will do a more thorough job than me but that should make him comfortable for now. See how he goes with the extra feed and call me, in a couple of weeks, if he's still looking poor. Watch him eat and see if he manages well, he shouldn't drop any food out of his mouth as he chews." Carrie made a mental note to get a dentist to visit soon and check them all.

As they left the barn Caleb said, "Can you spare us twenty minutes for a chat Jane, we have a proposition for you?"

"If I can eat my sandwich while we chat then yes, I'm due a break for lunch."

"I can heat you some soup if you like, that's what we're having?" offered Carrie.

"That sounds more inviting than a sandwich, made with dry bread, thanks."

They sat in the kitchen while the soup heated through. Carrie had some fresh rolls from the village shop, they were soon tucking in. Caleb began, "So Jane, a little bird told us that you might not be totally happy working for Scarton Practice. If that's the case, would you be interested to hear a proposition we have for you?"

"I'd definitely like to hear it, yes. If it means I can leave the practice, then I'll even forgive the 'little bird' for being indiscreet! I'm guessing it was Don? I'd like to hear what you have in mind."

Caleb assured her. "Don wasn't really indiscreet. He just suggested you might be interested in moving on, but that you had to remain local due to family ties. Please don't be mad at him, he was hoping he might help us both.

We've been impressed with your work for us, over the last few weeks, and we'll need a dedicated vet here at the farm in the future. We weren't thinking of taking anyone on for a year, but we'd like the person we take on to be you. If you're really unhappy at the Scarton practice, we'd like to offer you the position now, to start as soon as you wish. One proviso, as we don't have enough work for a full-time vet, is that you're willing to turn your hand to other things when there's no veterinary work. We were thinking of general work with the animals. Maybe exercising horses, or mucking out, I know you said you ride horses. We can agree on a salary that reflects your qualifications now and discuss it again when you're needed full time as a vet.

The other option is for you to work here, part-time, and use the facilities here, for your own clients, the rest of the time. We have plans for a veterinary centre, which will be built as soon as we have permission. You could have input into its internal design and have a purpose-built surgery to use for us, and for your own clients. When the work here eventually needs you full time, you can give up your clients. Does any of this sound like something you'd be interested in?"

"Wow, that all sounds way too good to be true, are you sure you want me, there are loads of better qualified vets who would jump at the chance of working here, especially if they had some say in the setting up of the surgery."

"We want someone we can work alongside. Some-one we can talk to and get along with. We both feel

140

you're approachable and would make a good team member. It's about personality far more than top qualifications for us. We feel you're the sort of person who'd go the extra mile. You strike us as the sort of sensible person, who'd happily admit you don't know all the answers. I'm guessing you'd also keep on researching until you did know the answers. Those are qualities that no qualification can manufacture. We want you."

Jane replied, "I'm flattered, and I'm very keen to find a new position, but I can't afford a huge salary drop, I have a mortgage. That's why I'm stuck where I am. I couldn't expect to be paid enough as a yard hand to pay my bills. I also need the security of a regular income, which is why I don't have the courage to set up my own practice. Whilst I'd dearly love to work here, in any capacity, I don't think I can afford to."

Carrie spoke up, "We've done a bit of research, to try and work out a good basic wage for a youngish vet. We'd happily pay you the sort of figures we found, it just depends how generous your current employers are, whether we can match what you earn now. We wrote an annual figure down, when we were researching, if I show you, you can say if you could live on that amount, without having to tell us what you earn now." Carrie handed her a slip of paper with a figure on it.

Jane looked at the slip of paper and said. "This figure would be about right for a full-time vet, it's even a bit more than I'm earning currently, but what about now, when you only need me a yard hand most of the time, you can't pay me that much now?"

"Why not?" asked Caleb.

Jane looked confused. "Why not? – because it's well above the pay rate for a general help. I don't want charity, I want to earn my pay."

Carrie countered. "What if you considered it as a retainer? We want you, and are prepared to pay you now, to ensure we get you as a vet when we need you."

"I need to think about this, it seems so unusual. Can I let you know?"

"Yes of course," said Carrie. "How about you come back with your microchip reader in a day or two, we can scan the ponies for chips and discuss it more then. Chat to Don, he's coming on board with us, as our farrier, and having the leeway to keep his old clients too. Juan has been on the payroll for weeks, so talk to him as well, get an idea if we are genuine and OK to work for. Shall I give Juan a shout so you can chat, we'll go out and leave you to it?"

Jane agreed and Juan came in for a chat. Once Caleb had made Juan and Jane a drink, he and Carrie went to check the horses and left them chatting. "Do you think Juan will be nice about us?"Giggled Carrie. "He might say we're unhinged or something."

Caleb laughed. "Let's hope we're seen as eccentric, rather than unhinged, shall we?"

By the time they returned from the fields, Jane had gone and Juan had returned to the job he was doing. "Go and ask him how the chat went, Caleb, the suspense is killing me."

"I can't go and interrogate the poor man, just wait and see what happens."

Later Juan came into the kitchen and, luckily for Carrie, started the conversation himself. "That Jane's a lovely girl, she came out to the cows once or twice.

143

She's much easier to talk to than the other guy they sent. He made you feel you were wasting his time, mostly. I think I set her mind at rest, that you're good to work for. She's scared to take the chance I think, hopefully seeing me happy here helped, anyhow."

"Thanks for talking to her Juan, we'd love her to work here. Fingers crossed," said Carrie.

Later, in bed, Carrie and Caleb discussed their day. "Do you think Jane will join us?" asked Carrie.

"I hope so, she seems desperate to leave the practice, so let's hope that gives her the courage to take the risk. If she does, we'll have three staff members. We'd better rescue some more animals to keep them busy."

"How are we going to find all these animals, no one knows we're here yet? I assume we should contact the local council or someone and register as a sanctuary. Do we need licences and things?"

"Babs started to talk me through it last time I phoned her, I don't think we need to do much more until the building work is finished. Let's concentrate on that for now. If animals come to us, we can take them but we won't advertise yet. My lawyers have put feelers out with the council, and other relevant people, so some of it is going on behind the scenes already. Let's see if the planning application goes through, without a fight, first."

"I've thought of one thing I'd like to add to the farm, if you're OK with it. We really need an outdoor arena to ride in. If we want to rehabilitate horses and get them fit, we need to be able to ride them regularly. Hacking out is good exercise but they'll need to work in the arena as well, to train them. Is there somewhere we could fit one in? I wondered about near the old barns."

"Let's give it more thought tomorrow," said Caleb, rolling towards her and kissing her neck. "I have something much more important on my mind right now!"

Chapter 11

Building

Jane returned to the farm two days later and accepted their job offer. She had to give a months' notice at the practice but planned to start at Cliff Top at the end of November.

Jane brought her microchip reader and they discovered the three chestnut ponies were Milly, Molly and Mandy. They wrote detailed descriptions on how to tell which was which, but they still got confused most of the time. Bud and Carl were easier to remember as Bud had a single black hoof and three white ones while Carl had four white hooves. They wrote down which was which, for their new owner.

*   *   *   *   *

One morning, a few weeks later, a letter from the planners arrived. Amazingly, they were in support of the development of the Sanctuary and had given permission for the barns to be built. The application paperwork had shown detailed computer-generated images of what the two new barn buildings would be like. They were both to be fully enclosed with solid walls all round, more like buildings on an industrial estate than an agricultural barn. The design showed them both with slatted wooden cladding on the outside to make them blend in better. Both buildings also had huge banks of solar panels on their roof, which impressed the council. The only real stipulation that the planners made, was that they must plan a comprehensive planting programme to soften the look of the buildings, and they must submit the plan for inspection and then stick to it. Building work could begin. Caleb was on the phone to the steel building manufacturers that morning. He had already had quotes, so they knew what he wanted. The manufacturers offered an erection service, once the concrete bases were laid. Caleb called the local building contractors he had chosen, to come and start the groundwork as soon as possible. Winter was fast approaching and he wanted things moving.

For the next few months, the farm looked more like a building site from the road. Once the concrete bases were laid, luckily just before the first frosts, the steel frames of the buildings went up really fast. The contractors who renovated the courtyard were booked to fit out the insides of the building once the steel shells were constructed.

Bud and Carl went to their new home in November. Pat, their new owner, seemed really nice and was thrilled at how well the pair looked. Caleb and Carrie waved goodbye to them with mixed emotions. They were really pleased the cobs had found a good home but also knew they would miss them. Carrie asked Pat to send photos or video when she got them working. She wanted to see them harnessed up as a pair and pulling a cart together, they would look stunning.

Some of the remaining horses started to come into the stables at night by the end of November. The three ponies and Monkey stayed out mostly, only coming in on really wet and rough nights. They were bred to take cold weather in their stride. Bilbo, Cloud, who was looking much better, Noddy and Jaffa were kept in the stables every night and turned out to graze every day.

A few days after the horses started coming in at

night Jane started working for the farm. She was able to help Carrie with the mucking out and between them they started working with all the horses, except Cloud and Monkey, to get them ready to be ridden again. Jaffa was calm and obliging. They risked sitting on him very quickly, and, within a week, they took him and Bilbo out for a hack around the farm. Both horses behaved beautifully and Jaffa seemed to really enjoy being ridden out. It looked like Caleb had found a good horse.

All they could do with the three little ponies was lunge them, neither Carrie or Jane were small enough to ride them. They reacted as if they had done it all before and behaved well. Noddy was just big enough for them to ride so they tried him out one day. He was a bit shocked at being asked to work after all this time and showed his displeasure by trying to buck Carrie off. Once he realised she was not going to give in, he slowly became more willing, and after half an hour of gentle riding round the field, he was behaving much better. They decided he needed working every day, to get him behaving well. The others had been so good, they felt a once or twice a week workout would be all they needed to keep them going over the winter. After they had tried them all they got into a routine of hacking out each morning with one of them on Noddy and one on one of the others. The small ponies got lunged, whenever the ground was dry enough to do it without cutting up the grass too much. When they had time Carrie and Caleb took Bilbo and Jaffa for a ride in the afternoons too. All the horses were becoming fitter and their feet were all back to being healthy, it would soon be time to look for new homes for them.

By early December the buildings were both up, although they were empty shells. The solar panels were fitted and waiting to be wired in. The plan was that they would power the new buildings, with mains connection for backup when necessary. They could even sell power back to the grid if there was an excess. Caleb hoped to fit solar panels to the two older barns eventually, to power the house and the lighting in those barns.

Chapter 12

Partying

The November bonfire party/house warming celebration finally happened in the middle of December. They decided to have an afternoon party for the locals, followed by an evening party for a few close friends. For the evening do, Caleb had invited four other actors, who'd been friends of his for years, and Stephen and Ellie, who were old college friends of Carrie's. Stephen also just happened to be a colleague of Caleb's. Carrie had invited Sally and Terry and her old house-mates, Gregg and Dave.

For the afternoon party, Carrie had put an open invitation to all the Santon villagers on a poster in the village shop window. She and Caleb were getting quite friendly with the lady who ran the shop. They explained to her there would be a big bonfire and free hog roast and burgers for anyone who would like to come. There would be a chance to see around the outside of the new buildings and a quick talk on what they were planning to do with them. They were invited to come at 2pm and stay for a couple of hours. Carrie explained, after that, the Sanctuary would not be open to the public, but that local village groups could arrange a tour, once the building work was all finished and they had some animals. The shop lady listened carefully to all they had to tell her, then said, "It's a lovely idea and people will come, but you do realise most of them will want to see Mr Kirkmichael more than anything? Word's got around that you're living there, most people will just want an autograph or a photo."

Caleb laughed. "You're right and I'm expecting that, but, if it gets a few of them interested in what we're doing, that's no bad thing. That's why we've limited it to two hours, I can happily sign and pose for that long. We've ordered a big sign, with the name of the sanctuary and a phone number. I'll pose in front of that, every photo will be an advert for the farm. Can you think of anywhere else a poster would be seen?"

"You could put one in the church, if you ask the vicar. Maybe the village hall as well, I can put one up there if you like, I'm at Pilates tonight." Caleb thanked her and gave her another poster. They browsed for a few bits to eat, then went off to call at the vicarage. They found the vicar in and introduced themselves. He laughed and said he knew at least one of them by sight. They showed him the poster and asked him if he would tell his congregation about the gathering. He was a young and switched on vicar, and he grinned as he said, "I'll display your poster and tell everybody I meet about it, on one condition."

"What's that?" asked Carrie.

"Our church is in desperate need of repair and funds are only trickling in slowly. Can we go around the crowds and shake a bucket at them, while they are at your party? Every little really helps."

"Of course, we aren't fundraising, so you'll have no competition," said Carrie. "How much do you need to raise?"

"Well, anything we get from your do will be wonderful, but overall, we need around sixty thousand pounds to do the work. We've managed just over ten thousand so far. It still feels a long way to go, but I have faith."

Carrie could feel Caleb thinking behind her. "How about you ask a few of your congregation if they'd agree to be stewards for the afternoon at our party?" he said. "They can shake their buckets and steer people to the places they're meant to be. We can ply them with food, and I'll extend an invitation to them to come up to the house after the other villagers have gone home. They can have a chat with me and a cup of tea. Obviously, they can have autographs and photos too, if they're interested. I can even promise there maybe a couple of other famous faces to meet at the house, by the time they leave, as some of my film industry friends are visiting us that evening. If they would do us this favour, I'll make a donation to the church fund that will definitely move you a step closer. We'd really like to feel part of the village and hopefully this party will help that. What do you think?"

"Sounds like a great idea, I'll pick some trustworthy people, how many do you think?"

"Up to ten would be good, if there are enough volunteers. I'll give you my mobile number, you can let me know if you've found some willing victims! We can discuss details once we know a few people are happy to help."

"I'll be the first volunteer, I'm a sucker for a film star! And I will persuade others, hell-fire and damnation make great bargaining tools! Can we expect to see you both in Church on Sunday now we're friends?"

"One thing at a time Vicar, one thing at a time!" laughed Caleb.

As they walked back to the farm Carrie was deep in thought. "Do you think you can make them a good donation? It really is a beautiful old church. It might make all the difference to how we're perceived by the village too. Added to that, he was the cutest vicar I've ever seen, I bet he gets the ladies packed in the pews."

Caleb stopped and gave her a look. "I'm going to have to stop allowing you off the farm my girl, I can't have you throwing yourself at anything in trousers, it's unseemly!"

Carrie giggled, "I only have eyes for you my love, and anyway, he was wearing a dress!"

Caleb chased her up the road, laughing as they went.

155

When they reached the farm, Caleb took her in his arms and said. "I was thinking we could donate all the money they need for the church, what do you think? Is that too much, will it seem too brash? I think the sale on the Hollywood house is going through finally, so it's not like we would miss the money. I just want to get the balance right between helping and seeming like I'm buying favour."

Carrie kissed his cheek and said, "How about if you gave them forty thousand, that way they still have ten thousand to raise, but they could probably start the work. Also, they know they can raise ten thousand, as they already have, so it will seem achievable. If they are still struggling to raise the last bit by next year, you could donate the rest."

"You always have the best solutions, that's genius, I knew I was marrying you for a reason. Shall we ask the cute vicar to marry us? He might be prepared to do an alfresco wedding here? He did seem a fun chap, despite the cute looks, and the dress – which I'm sure isn't what you call it, isn't it a cassock or something?"

"He was sweet, it's worth asking him, it would be nice to be married by someone we know, not some faceless official. Neither of us is a Christian though, will he mind, are there rules?"

"We can ask him when he's here for the party. He can only say no. I'll tell him about the donation first, that should put him in a good mood!"

* * * * *

The day of the bonfire party dawned bright and fair, which worried Carrie. The chances of it staying that way all day were pretty slim in December. Thankfully the forecast was for cold, dry and windless weather, right through into the night. The sun was shining and the frost was melting by 9am. In the front field, near the pond, a twenty-foot high pile of hedge cuttings, fallen trees and general wood rubbish was waiting to be lit. The pond had been carefully fenced off to stop anyone upsetting the ducks, or drowning and spoiling the afternoon. The catering firm, that would feed the villagers, was booked and should be arriving soon to start the two hog roasts. Thankfully they were supplying every-thing, including a constant supply of burgers, hog roast, deep-fried mushrooms and cooked peppers for vegetarians, and those wanting extras. The caterers were also supplying fruit juice in biodegradable

157

cups. No crockery or cutlery was allowed, all the food would be served in easily biodegradable serviettes. Bins had been put out everywhere in the hope that they would be used.

When the caterers had asked how many they were catering for, Carrie had panicked. They looked up the population of the village on google and were horrified to see it was in the high hundreds. They explained the problem to the caterers and they were wonderful. They said they would bring a freezer box van, full of supplies, and keep them frozen until they needed them, that way they would have plenty, but there would be no waste of burgers or buns if they weren't needed. They couldn't do that with the vegetables, but they brought plenty. Obviously, the hog roasts may run out quickly but they took hours to cook so they just had to hope the two whole pigs were enough.

Jane and Don had volunteered to see to the horses, so Carrie could finish preparing for the afternoon. Caleb and Juan had found the sign for the sanctuary and knocked its posts into the ground in the middle of the field, this was Caleb's photo and autograph area, he had an old trestle table and an even older chair to sit on. Juan would be in charge of keeping people away from the farmhouse and the horses. He would have two or three of the vicar's stewards to help, and he was taking his duties very seriously. They had hung gates across the drive up to the house, so that no one would think they could go that way. Juan wasn't satisfied and was still prowling the perimeter and checking for weak spots in his defences. The only parts of the farm that were open to the locals were the big front field, where the bonfire was, and the area around the new buildings, so people could take a closer look. The other stewards were tasked with keeping people moving around the buildings and keeping a general eye out for anyone sneaking into places they were not meant to be. There were three portable toilets at one side of the field and Carrie could not think of anything else they could prepare. Jane was happy to show people around the buildings and answer any questions they had. Don would talk to anyone in the field who had questions. Caleb would be fending off fans so he was unlikely to get a chance to talk to people about the sanctuary.

At 1.30pm people started queuing at the main gate. Juan and Don kept the gates closed until 1.45pm, then relented and let people in off the road. Everyone else was in place and everyone knew their

159

jobs. As the gates opened and people streamed in Caleb stood at his table and boomed out, in his best actor voice, "Gather round everyone and I'll tell you a bit about us." The ripple of excitement, when people saw who was shouting, was palpable. Carrie stood beside Caleb and watched the crowd form into an audience around him. He spoke clearly and briefly about what the sanctuary would be like, introduced Carrie and mentioned Don, Jane and Juan, who all got cheers from their village friends. He invited them to take a walk around the buildings and to have as much food as they wanted. Lastly, he announced that anyone wanting an autograph and a quick photo should come back to the table in fifteen minutes and form a queue. He and Carrie escaped into the nearest of the new buildings and watched the crowd out of the window. "How many do you think there are out there?" asked Carrie.

"Bloody millions!" said Caleb, but he looked pleased.

"Did you invite anyone from the press?" Carrie asked. "I only just thought about it."

"I did invite someone from the local paper, on the vicar's insistence, but I didn't want the nationals here poking around. They can take up the story after the local paper's had its scoop, if I'm still newsworthy. I've been out of the press for a few months now so I may be old news already."

Some people dispersed from around the table when Caleb disappeared, and went to look for food or to look around the buildings, but many just stayed. After a few minutes, they shuffled themselves back into a queue and patiently waited for Caleb to return. As Carrie watched many of them got DVDs out of their bags, ready to have them signed. Others had shiny new autograph books or notepaper.

After a few more minutes Caleb decided it was time to go and see his adoring fans. He and Carrie came out of the building, locking it behind them and started back towards the table and the queue, which was huge. People saw them coming straight away, a cheer went up from the crowd. Caleb took his seat, right beneath the Sanctuary sign, and smiled at the first fan. Carrie imagined Caleb would be all smiled out by the time he worked through this lot. The vicar appeared next to her and asked if he could help at all. Carrie suggested he marshal the fans into taking a quick photo after getting their autograph, so they could keep things moving. She hoped people's respect for his dog collar would help him persuade them to move along.

She was just thinking how well it was all going when she got a tap on the shoulder from a man holding a professional looking camera and a notebook. "Hi love, I hear you're Caleb's missus. I'm from the newspaper, ready to get a photo and a few words. Can we jump the queue do you think?"

Carrie wasn't sure she could face the wrath of the crowd, if they pushed in, so she caught the vicar's eye and called him over. As soon as he understood what was needed, he took control of his flock. "Mr Kirkmichael needs to take a quick press call, if you can all stand back from the good man, he will start signing again very shortly. The crowds parted in a very biblical way and the local journalist grabbed his opportunity for a photo of Caleb, Carrie and the vicar under the sign. He took a few words from Caleb about the farm and the day. Within five minutes Caleb was back signing autographs and smiling for the cameras. Carrie was full of gratitude. "Thank you so much, vicar, I wasn't sure I could command that sort of authority, that was wonderful."

"You're welcome Mrs Kirkmichael, it was my

162

pleasure, and please call me Julian, Vicar is what I am, not who I am." He gave her a very slightly flirty smile.

"Well then please call me Carrie, especially as Caleb and I aren't married yet. In fact, we were going to try and talk to you about that today, as well as the donation for the Church fund. I think any talking will have to wait until the crowds disperse though. Are you coming up to the house later with the other stewards?"

"I'll be there, don't you worry, I'd better get back to my shepherding duties now though, before Mr Kirkmichael gets mobbed."

Carrie looked around the field as she moved away. Everywhere she looked, people were eating and chatting happily, sitting on straw bales or just standing in groups. She turned and looked towards the buildings. Jane had a group of people around her and was talking to them, animatedly. Jane and the group disappeared behind the buildings with the locals looking enthralled by her words. As she walked across the field, she saw Don, also talking to a group of locals, looking totally happy and relaxed. Her heart nearly burst with pride and happiness for

163

him, he had come so far in such a short time. Within a few minutes she, herself, was engulfed in a group of villagers, all wanting to know about the farm. More importantly, they all wanted to know what it was like living with superstar Caleb Kirkmichael!

At around 3pm she saw movement by the bonfire and realised Juan was about to light it. She wandered over to check everyone was behind the rope, placed to keep people away from the flames. The stewards were doing a great job and everyone was being sensible.

For a few moments the bonfire just smouldered and smoked, Carrie wondered if it was going out. All of a sudden something caught light and there was a rush of flames shooting upwards. The sound of crackling wood and whine of burning sap filled the air. The comforting warmth started to radiate out into the field. People began gravitating towards the flames, enjoying the warmth and the smells as the fire grew. There were whoops and cheers from the children, as the fire cracked and popped. The light was fading from the sky now, which made the flames seem so bright and pretty as they jumped around. She felt an arm through hers as Don appeared by her side. He smiled at the fire and they just watched in silence. Jane appeared soon after and Don took her arm in his too. All three of them stood and just enjoyed the warmth from the fire seeping through their clothes. A while later, Juan joined them too. Carrie put her arm through his and they all had an unspoken team bonding moment. Carrie looked back at Caleb on his table, missing him suddenly. He only had a couple of people waiting now, he looked up and saw them, all standing together, and smiled proudly. He blew her a kiss as he posed for one last photo then headed their way. As he joined the team watching the fire, people were beginning to leave the field and head home. Many stopped and thanked them for a fun afternoon and some even offered to help clear up. The stewards all slowly gravitated to the fire, as the numbers of visitors reduced. Caleb turned and thanked them all for their sterling work. He reminded them to come to the house for a hot drink after the rest of the locals had left and they'd shut the gates.

Carrie, Jane and Don did a quick sweep of the field to pick up the worst of the litter, they were impressed how little there was. Caleb and the stewards politely herded the stragglers out and shut the gates. With all the paper waste burning on the bonfire they all sat and watched the flames for a few minutes. Once the paper was burnt up, and the fire was safe, they all headed back to the house for a nice cup of tea.

Chapter 13

Meeting

Jane and Don had found time to bring the horses into the stables and feed them. Carrie said a quick hello to them all and stood in the courtyard looking around. With horses peering out over stable doors, breath steaming, and the lights in the yard giving it a warm glow she could not think of anywhere she would rather be. Caleb was in the kitchen, entertaining the stewards with tales of his career when she walked in. He passed her a cuppa and hugged her tight. Turning back to everyone he said, "That went so much better than I expected, everyone was so nice, they all seemed ready to welcome us and the sanctuary here. Thanks again, to all of you, for your hard work. A special thanks to the future Mrs Kirkmichael here, who supports all my wild ideas." He kissed the top of her head as everyone smiled at them.

Carrie said, "I hope you all ate well this afternoon,

as I've nothing to offer you now, except my thanks for all your help. Who'd like Caleb to sign stuff, or do you want to have a photo with him? We probably ought to do it before his smile runs out, I think his face must be pretty sore already." Everyone, including the vicar and Jane, had photos with Caleb. Carrie asked them all for a group photo, all the helpers and her and Caleb. She set a shutter delay on her phone and propped it on a counter. She pressed the button and rushed to her spot in the group, she just managed to get still and smile before the shutter clicked. "Stay there while I check we got everyone." She looked at the shot, it looked fine but she wanted to be sure. "Just one more for luck," she said rushing back to her place again. "Thanks guys, that one's a good one." They all sat down in the sitting room sipping their drinks and chatting, half of them sitting on the floor as there was just one sofa and the chairs they had brought from the kitchen. Caleb signed a few bits of paper with nice little notes of thanks to those that wanted them. The vicar, Julian, was just preparing to head home when Caleb took him aside and gave him the cheque. They stood talking quietly for some time, Carrie wanted to join them but two of the stewards were quizzing her about the sanctuary and she didn't want to be rude and leave them. Caleb saw her across the room and smiled and blew her a kiss. He obviously had no intention of rescuing her!

Julian was just about to leave again, when there was a knock on the door and 4 people walked in. Carrie didn't know them so she guessed they were Caleb's friends. The men were all tall, dark and handsome and the lady was dressed for a dinner party, not an evening of sitting around a bonfire. Caleb rushed to greet them, hugging the men and kissing the lady on the cheek. He turned to the group and introduced his friends. "Carrie, Julian, stewards, Don, Jane, Juan meet my colleagues Bill Winter, Jim Besser and Julie and Martyn Silverdale. I'm sure the names and faces will be familiar. Guys, meet the wonderful team who have made this afternoon's event a huge success, including my beautiful fiancée Carrie." He put his arm around Carrie as she shook hands with the newcomers. The stewards seemed very quiet suddenly, Carrie suspected they knew who Caleb's friends were better than she did. Julian stepped forward and shook hands with each in turn. "It's a pleasure and a thrill to meet you all, but I'm afraid I must leave now. I'm sure you'll all have a pleasant evening." Caleb saw Julian out and when he returned the others were all preparing to leave too. "Shall we take a group photo before you all go, I'll send copies to you all afterwards." Everyone crowded into a huddle around the five actors and Carrie took the shots. Don offered to take one with her in, and Caleb insisted when she tried to resist. She joined the throng and more pictures were taken. One of the stewards asked, shyly, if he could have autographs and soon all the newcomers were scribbling away for them, even signing a sheet for Julian in his absence. Carrie showed the stewards out, once the signing was completed, and thanked them again for their support. With shouts of goodbye and thanks, they headed off down the drive. Caleb was making more coffee for their guests as she came back inside. He smiled and hugged her as she came to help. "Wow, what a day, I'm so pleased with how it went," he said as he held her. "Julian was speechless when I gave him the cheque, I think he shed a tear too. He said marrying us was the least he could do. Unfortunately, he isn't allowed to do it here, only in the church, do you want to do that, or use a registry office? Apparently, in this strange little country, we can only get married in a registered location. Our field just won't do I'm afraid."

She smiled up at her fiancé, who kissed her lightly on the lips. "That's a shame, but the church will be lovely, we can have the rest of the day back here afterwards. Shall we walk there and back or hire a coach for everyone?" They discussed the wedding more as they re-joined the others in the sitting room. There, the conversation was all about films and acting, of course. Carrie sat back and let the conversation flow around her without really listening. Don and Jane were quietly chatting in the corner of the room, they were staying for the evening, Juan had left with the stewards. She could see Caleb was really enjoying catching up on the news with his friends. She watched his handsome, animated face with wonder, he really was the most gorgeous man, how did she get so lucky? As if he had a sixth sense, he turned to look at her and winked. She winked back and smiled contentedly.

Sally, Terry, Gregg and Dave arrived twenty minutes later, singing Christmas Carols by the back door until Caleb let them in. They came into the sitting room full of good cheer and hugged Carrie from all directions. Carrie and the lads hadn't seen each other for months and she had really missed them. They all sat where they could as Caleb introduced the other guests. Sally suddenly noticed Caleb's actor friends and Carrie could see her excitement rise. Sally was an avid celebrity follower and gossip magazine reader. She plonked herself down next to Bill Winter and proceeded to chat to

171

him quite happily. Terry looked uncomfortable and stood next to Carrie not knowing where to put himself. Carrie took pity and led him over to meet Don and Jane, explaining who they were and introducing Terry to them. Don chatted away about horseshoes and hoof health with Jane adding her perspective and Terry asking questions of both of them.

Carrie was just realising she was the only one with no one to chat to when Julie Silverdale came over to her smiling. "Hi Carrie, we've heard so much about you from Caleb, it is nice to meet you at last. I have to say, he looks younger and happier than I've seen him for years. You're obviously a good tonic! Farming life is suiting him too, much to our surprise."

Carrie smiled, "It's lovely to meet you all too."

Julie continued, "Martyn told me we were coming here tonight, but he forgot to mention we might be sitting outside in December. I dressed to kill, force of habit, but I will perish out there like this. Stupid thing is, I am a keen fell walker when I get a chance. I have plenty of warm and practical clothes that I could have worn if Martyn had remembered to tell me. Do you have a warm coat or something I could borrow?"

Carrie laughed and said, "Of course, why don't we go upstairs and see what I have that fits. You are much taller than me and much thinner, but no one will see you in the dark so we can make do."

They headed to the wardrobe in the master bedroom and Carrie pulled out some warm jogging bottoms and a thick fleece. She found a long, thick pair of boot socks, which would bridge the gap between Carrie's short legged joggers and Julie's mile long legs. As an afterthought, Carrie added a scarf and hat. Laughing, Julie tried them all on and declared she would be warm as toast, even if she looked frightful. "What size are your feet Julie, I may have a spare pair of warm boots you can borrow too."

"I'm a size five mostly."

"Oh, well I'm a size six, so with thick socks, you should be OK, we'll find them when we go downstairs."

Just as the party were preparing to head out to the bonfire, Stephen and Ellie arrived, looking flustered and apologising for being late. Hugs all round followed, with introductions for Don and Jane. Everyone had found big warm coats and good boots from their cars. Julie did a pirouette for them all, looking like a scarecrow that had a growth spurt, in Carries warm but ill-fitting clothes. They all clapped and whistled as if she were a model, then laughed as she took a bow. With a huge torch to light the way, they trooped around the pond and headed towards the warmth of the glowing embers. There were enough straw bales for everyone to sit on, placed near the fire. Carrie noticed that the caterers were still there in the corner of the field and she could smell cooking. Caleb saw where she was looking and whispered, "We deserve some food too, so I arranged for them to stay and feed us." Carrie quietly thanked the heavens for her fiancé, she hadn't even thought about feeding this lot! Caleb was a natural host, which was just as well. She knew they had wine and beer stashed near the pond and a huge pile of marshmallows for toasting, but the thought of a meal hadn't even crossed her mind.

In twos and threes, the friends approached the catering trailer and chose from the small menu. As well as burgers they offered cod and chips, sausages, chicken nuggets and other traditional chip shop fare.

Everyone seemed very happy with the range of unsophisticated food and they all tucked in. Caleb was sitting with the two younger male actors and howls of laughter could be heard from the three of them. Carrie sat with Martyn and Julie and they all chatted about Caleb's past and what their plans were now. Julie asked, "Will Caleb act again do you think?" Carrie thought about it before answering, "I haven't seen much sign of him missing it, for the last six months, but seeing him now, with Bill and Jim, he is a different person. I think he may have missed the buzz more than he realises. I hope he still gets offered roles, I'd hate for him to be written off. I know he is loving this life but we all need a bit of variety to fire us up. Do you think film people will still want him?"

Martyn laughed, "They will be knocking down your door if they think they have a role he might accept. I don't think you need to worry on that score. We all thought he was finished with films for good. If you think he's open to offers, I'll keep my ear to the ground. A hint, in the right place, will be all it takes for him to work again when the role and the time is right. He can always refuse, but it's good for the ego to be wanted."

Carrie replied, "That's good to hear, I don't want to push him either way. I love him being here all the time, with me, and it would be easy to dissuade him for that reason. But I also realise that acting is part of his soul and I would never, intentionally, hold him back from that. He must make his own choices."

Julie hugged Carrie close. "You have no idea how happy you've made me. We knew Caleb was totally in love with you, we were worried that this new life was to please you, and not what he really wanted. I feel really happy that you won't stand in his way if he wants to act. He is such a good actor and that comes from his soul, he lives the part. To see him give that up was heartbreaking to us. I can see he is very happy here, but now I know the acting door is still open, if he wants it, I am really relieved and happy for you both."

Carrie wondered if she'd really given Caleb's acting career enough thought these last blissful months. "Thank you for caring so much for him. Please believe me that the farm is totally Caleb's dream, not mine. I would have followed him any- where. He hasn't even mentioned acting for months, but now you've made me see it from both sides, I'll make sure he knows I'm behind him all the way, if he chooses to act again. The more staff we have here the easier it will be for him to take time away, so he can leave for a few months and still know he has all this to come back to. Hopefully, that will give him the best of both worlds." Carrie hugged Julie again, glad to have found a friend who could explain the parts of Caleb's life that were hidden to her.

Carrie moved around the circle of bales talking to friends, old and new. She joined Caleb, Bill and Jim for a while, enjoying Caleb's obvious pride in her, as they chatted away. She then moved on to chat with Dave and Gregg, who were talking with Don and Jane about Elver. As she sat down Dave gave her a lovely hug and said, "The house is still a bit empty without you Carrie, although the cooking has improved." He winked and Gregg nearly spat his beer out.

Carrie grinned, "You never complained when I was living there, you could've taken over my share of the cooking duties anytime."

"What, and miss out on 'one hundred varieties of stew', never," replied Dave.

"I can't help it if I only know how to do stews,

they have everything in them anyway, what more do you need?"

Gregg joined the banter, "Yours definitely had everything in them, I remember one Monday stew that contained chopped up Yorkshire puddings from the Sunday roast I cooked."

Sally and Terry joined them and they all reminisced about their times together. Carrie told them quietly that she and Caleb were planning a summer wedding. Gregg suddenly dropped the bombshell that he and Dave should have a summer wedding next year too. Dave's face was a picture in the firelight, this was obviously news to him. He pounced on Gregg and questioned him, "Is this real, are you ready, finally, can I plan, Gregg I love you."

Carrie and the others were laughing and patting them both on the back. Gregg looked sheepish but confirmed to Dave that he was serious and agreed to start planning as soon as they got home. They all watched with a tear in their eye as Dave threw himself on Gregg for a huge kiss. "Where's my ring then, fiancé, I need a big fat diamond, like Carries!" Gregg looked bashful, "I thought we could choose them together." Dave kissed him again. "Just perfect, did I tell you I loved you?"

Caleb came over, to see what the fuss was about, and immediately announced the engagement to the others at the top of his voice. Everyone cheered and clapped and came over to talk to the lads. Soon everyone was talking together, swapping engagement stories and wedding ideas. The lads' announcement had brought them all together and the rest of the evening was spent like they were all old friends. Don looked a little outside his comfort zone contemplating a same-sex marriage, but he handled the new situation with empathy and warmth once he realised that Dave and Gregg had the same dreams and love as anyone. Jane hugged them both and then returned to Don's side and hugged him too. Don looked as happy as Carrie had ever seen him, as he stood in Jane's arms. The drinks flowed as toasts to Dave and Gregg, Carrie and Caleb and the sanctuary followed. Caleb grabbed the stash of marshmallows and found sticks for everyone and the next half hour was a sticky mess, of melted sugar and minor burns, as they toasted in a different way. Sally was feeling a little sick by the end, she ate so many. The evening finally ended, as the fire got so low that the cold crept in, and people were ready to move. Everyone was offered coffee, but the pull of sitting in a nice warm car with the heater on won, and all the guests left to make their different journeys. Carrie had noticed that everyone had been good, and each car had a dedicated driver. Jane was driving a quietly merry Don home, Bill had abstained all evening saying he was getting fit for a new role and Sally was sober knowing she had to work early in the morning. The lads shared a lift with Sally and Terry, which was just as well as they were now plastered, from celebrating their upcoming nuptials. Carrie and Caleb stood waving them all off, then did a quick check around the yard saying goodnight to the horses. "Carrie, I love you so much, and that was a perfect day," Caleb said as they stood arm in arm looking at Bilbo over his stable door. "I can't believe Dave and Gregg's announcement, it's wonderful."

"I don't think Dave could believe it either, Gregg just blurted it out, mid-conversation. Dave had to get Gregg to confirm he was serious before he dared to celebrate. I'm so happy for them."

After a few quiet moments Carrie continued, "Caleb, you do know that anytime you want to go back to acting, I'll support you all the way, don't you? I know you said you'd give it a year, but, if the right role comes up, I'll be really happy for you to go. We have staff now, friends, I won't be alone like before. I might even be able to go with you for some of the time. I'd like to understand more about that part of your life."

Caleb kissed her gently. "I'm the luckiest man in the world. Thank you. And thank you for knowing I needed to hear that tonight, you are amazing."

They finished up and went inside, both feeling that they had learnt something new about their friends and themselves that day.

Chapter 14

Developing

As January came, the fitting out of the new buildings started. The materials were arriving daily and Jane and Caleb were in constant brainstorming sessions, to make sure it was coming together as they wanted. Jane had some great ideas for the quarantine area as well as the veterinary areas. They realised early on that the buildings were tall enough for two storeys inside, so a mezzanine area had been created for offices and toilets in both, leaving the whole ground floor areas of the buildings free for animal use. Lifts were fitted for disabled use. They also doubled up as freight lifts, so that some of the upstairs areas could also be used to store equipment.

In the vet building a large area, with big sliding doors, had been left empty for future development as a horse operating theatre. For now, it could be used to examine and treat horses and bigger animals in a clean environment. The front reception area didn't need to be big, they were not a walk-in centre, but space was left to expand it, in case they decided that the vets would take on local clients in future. The front of the ground floor had six big rooms set aside as consultation rooms and small animal surgeries. The rest of the ground floor was to be fitted with large dog and cat pens, as well as a few larger penned areas, to take any type of animal that needed help. The space was divided into enclosed rooms with insulated walls and ceilings to keep the temperature even and the noise levels contained. As many of the pens as could, had access to outside yards, with closable doors for warmth. What was left of the space was for storage and expansion as needed. The whole huge area was insulated really thoroughly to help regulate the temperature. Heating was fitted to both buildings, using a similar green system to the one they planned to use in the house, which involved laying huge amounts of pipe under the soil in the next-door field. There was an MVHR system to recondition the air and reclaim any heat for reuse. They fitted electric heaters for really cold days as a top up.

The quarantine building was also divided into well insulated and sealed rooms, for veterinary procedures and pens. This time, each pen was fully isolated from the next to minimise the spread of germs. The larger pens, big enough for horses, were connected to outside spaces which were also fully walled so there was no horse to horse contact. There was a really large open space at the back of this building, still walled and roofed with huge roller doors on the end. Some of this space was for future expansion, but Don could use part of it for his storage and workshop. The dividing wall was again fully sealed and clad to make sure his area wasn't exposed to any germs from the quarantine area and everything was very fireproof. He had room to set up a small forge near the door, with a special fan and piping that allowed the fumes to be ducted out of the building. His forge was gas-fired so it was not very smoky. Horses from the farm could be shod within the building, out of the weather. He could store all the stuff he needed to go out and shoe other people's horses as well. It was the best space he had ever had and he intended to use it fully, doing some blacksmithing, making things out of metal, the old-fashioned way with heat and a hammer.

Juan had proved invaluable, as they knew he would, through the whole process. If they needed something done, he knew a local with that skill. If they needed to purchase something obscure, he knew where to look locally. His practical outlook saved them making a good few bad decisions with the building work too. He seemed to see what was needed in every area and tell them if they were not thinking the problem through properly. He really came out of his shell and would shower Caleb with ideas for improvements, or time saving measures, every week. Caleb ended up having to jot them down in a notebook he carried around so he did not forget any.

Jane seemed so happy and carefree now she had left the Scarton practice, she worked very hard and found jobs to do before anyone else had thought of them. She was loving the horse work, especially the riding, and she and Carrie were building a good bond. If there was any slight question over a horse's health, she was in there, examining and offering advice. She was looking forward to more veterinary challenges but was quite content for now. Planning the new buildings with Caleb was exciting and rewarding. Caleb was really good at listening to her and incorporating anything she suggested if it was at all possible. Jane and Juan had also had some good chats about the practicalities of the designs. Juan had never met a woman with such a practical mind and, despite his natural reticence, she and he became great buddies. They were a force to be reckoned with if they were not listened to. Caleb definitely listened when they came up with ideas together, he wouldn't dare ignore them, but he loved it.

By April almost everything in the new buildings was finished and preparations were underway to start on the house renovations. Carrie and Caleb were planning to move into a massive American style motor home, that Caleb had rented through his film contacts. It had probably been a dressing room for a film star at some point. It was huge and immaculate. Caleb had it parked inside the machinery barn, having moved the rest of the machinery to the other end to make space. It was under cover of the barn roof so they had a roofed space outside to sit on warm evenings. This was likely to be their home for most of the summer. Their plan to move into the village and rent a house, while their own house was renovated, had changed. They couldn't bear to leave the farm, even to sleep. The camper van, that Carrie had called Winnie, had everything they needed, including a king-sized bed. They emptied the house and put all their furniture and bits in the quarantine storeroom and moved straight in. The contractors were due to start on the house in a week and Caleb was beside himself with excitement. He had planned a grand updating of the house with all the modern, energy saving gadgets he could squeeze in, but made sure they were all invisible and the old house still kept its simple charm. His aim was that, apart from decoration and a new bathroom or two, no one would know the work had been done. The old house would be stripped right back in many places, to enable fitting a new underfloor heating system downstairs and a ducted air system upstairs. With these systems, plus new plumbing, electrics and insulation, not much stayed untouched. There were a few structural repairs to do while it was stripped back, woodworm to eradicate and roof trusses to strengthen, where damp had got in and rotted them. Caleb had instructed the contractors that anything badly rotted must be replaced with similar materials and everything that could be saved should be. The roof tiles were lovely and matched the courtyard so they were being kept and reused, with a few reclaimed ones to replace any that were broken. Apart from a couple of walls around an en suite bathroom, they were keeping the layout as it was. They already loved it, so why change things? Carrie had loved all the ideas Caleb came up with and had chosen most of the colour schemes herself so they were both happy with the changes. The only room that would be minimally affected was the kitchen, which was heated by its own Aga and did not need to connect to the new heating system. The kitchen had obviously been updated in recent years and already had new plumbing and units. At least everyone should be able to make tea!

Through the spring Caleb and Carrie watched their beloved house slowly stripped back to basics. The roof came off, the wood was repaired, water-proofing and insulation were added and the tiles were refitted. The ground source heat pump arrived and the groundworks for the great lengths of piping began in front of the house, luckily there was a paddock on one side so their sweet little garden was not disturbed. There were days and days when nothing obvious changed as the men worked inside the house. Carrie decided she would leave the inspections to Caleb as she found it quite upsetting seeing the house in a state of disrepair.

Living in 'Winnie' was fun, 'she' had a good heating system and was already wired for mains electricity, they only had to run a cable to a socket in the barn and they were warm, could cook and had good lights. Winnie had an electric cooker and fridge, they dragged their fridge freezer from the house into the barn for extra food storage too. Winnie's shower and toilet were amazing, they were definitely glamping. The bedroom area was walled off, along with the shower room but the rest was all open plan and fitted out to a very high spec. It was more like a posh hotel room really, just no room service! As Winnie had to be returned to her owner, nice and clean, in a few months, they made a rule of no work clothes or boots inside her. They set up a corner of the barn, with drapes to hide their modesty, so they could change into clean clothes each evening when they finished work. It was cold comfort getting changed in a draughty barn, they got pretty good at dressing quickly. There was an area next to Winnie in the barn, where they were able to make tea, and sit and chat with the staff, with a patio heater for the really cold days. By the time they moved in, a washing machine and drier had been plumbed into both the Quarantine building and the Veterinary Building, so doing the washing was possible, just a bit of a faff.

Luckily the weather in mid-April was warm and dry, so the horses didn't need to come into their stables at night anymore. The grass was growing really fast and the problem of over-fat ponies started again. Juan was already planning to get hay off the best fields soon. He cut the small paddocks, that

Carrie needed for the over-fat ponies and cobs really early. It made short hay, but it meant they could all graze a bit more safely on what was left. With all of the horses outside day and night, there was more time for riding and other jobs.

Carrie had long chats with Babs about how to re-home the horses that were fit enough. It was only Monkey and Cloud who they decided to keep, along with Bilbo and Jaffa of course. Monkey was staying because everyone loved him, and Cloud was old and deserved a comfy retirement. Babs called Carrie one day with a proposal. The old riding school that the horses had been rescued from was now under new ownership and starting to give lessons again. Babs wondered if any of their horses would be suitable to return there. Carries first response was an emphatic No. She felt they might remember being so hungry there and not settle. Also, she dreamed of them all finding private homes, with people who would love them, rather than a commercial yard, where they would be one of many. Babs arranged for Carrie and Caleb to visit the riding school and see for themselves how well it was being run. They had a good afternoon, chatting with the new owners and watching a couple of riding lessons. When they got home, they talked about what they had seen and whether the life of the ponies would be better there than at the farm. In the end, it was Caleb who said, "They'll teach hundreds of new riders how to look after horses properly if they are there. Maybe we should see them as ambassadors for us and Babs. They are a testament to what can be achieved with the right care. We can visit, and Babs will keep a regular eye. She has already allowed two of her horses to go there. I think we should be guided by her."

Carrie agreed, reluctantly. They arranged for the riding school owners to come to the farm and see the horses. Unfortunately, Caleb had to go to London on the day they were coming, so Carrie and Jane showed them around and let them meet the horses ready for re-homing. The three chestnut ponies were an immediate hit, the school was short of well-behaved small ponies. Carrie and Jane lunged them so they could see their paces and watch how they behaved. The ponies all behaved beautifully.

Lastly, they looked at Noddy. Carrie was very honest about his bucking when they first started riding him. She told them that, since being ridden every day, he had behaved well. Jane rode him around the field to show him off and then the lady from the riding school rode him too. When she got on, Carrie watched him closely to see if he was going to try her out, by misbehaving. His ears were flicking as he felt someone new on his back and he looked a bit tense. The woman gently rode him around the field in a walk and then asked for a trot. Noddy's ears went back and he swished his tail sharply, but then he trotted on as if nothing was bothering him. He trotted in both directions and then cantered beautifully calmly around the field. Carrie muttered thanks to the gods that they had done so much work with him, it would have been very embarrassing if he had bucked her off.

When all four of the available animals had been viewed, the riding school owner asked if she could take them all. She felt the chestnut ponies would be useful for beginners to learn to ride on. Noddy would be a good challenge for children who could ride a bit already. He was also big enough for a small adult, which made him more versatile. The woman was very impressed and said she would be giving Babs a good donation, as payment for the ponies. She would tell all her clients about their work at the sanctuary. Carrie didn't know whether to feel sad or happy that the horses were going. She tried hard to remain business-like, while they sorted out the paperwork and loaded all the ponies into the riding school's lorry. Babs had supplied all the re-homing paperwork, as the ponies officially still belonged to her Sanctuary.

Once the lorry left the farm, Carrie sat on a grass bank and cried her heart out. Jane sat with her and shed a tear herself. They had both got particularly fond of Noddy over the months, and the ponies were just sweet. "I know this is what we are supposed to be doing, but it's really hard to part with them after all this time," Carrie sniffed, "I feel really unsure about sending them back to that place, even though the new owners seem really nice."

Jane smiled, "I feel really sad too, but happy as well. They will have good, full lives and help the next generation to learn to respect animals. That has to be the best thing to remember. Loads of kids will learn to love ponies by loving them. If they stayed here we'd love them, but no one else would see them."

Carrie wiped her eyes and smiled. "I know you're right and I agree, but the fields will feel empty tonight."

As they walked back to the house Caleb was just

arriving home. He took one look at Carrie's face and pulled her in for a big hug. "Oh sweetie, you look so sad, did they take some of the ponies? I'm so sorry I wasn't here."

"I'm OK, my logical head knows it's a good thing, it's just my emotional head that's missing them already."

"I thought I saw their lorry, as I came through the village, have they only just gone? Who did they take?" Caleb asked.

"Everyone," wailed Carrie, suddenly overcome with sadness again.

Jane, who had been watching them hugging with a wistful look, took over the story. "They wanted all three of the ponies and Noddy too. The little git behaved himself perfectly this afternoon. I kind of hoped he would play up and put them off, but he didn't. I'm going to miss him. We both know it's good and right that they move on, it just sucks right now!"

Caleb managed to put his arm around Jane whilst still holding Carrie tight. "Come on my lovely, kind and caring team, lets overdose on tea and talk it through."

They headed for Winnie and the kettle. Don appeared just as the kettle was boiling. Still looking tearful, Jane explained the afternoon's events to him. He surprised everyone, including Jane, by pulling her in for a big hug and saying. "You sweet, wonderful, contrary woman, isn't this what we are working here for?" Jane looked up at him smiling and he kissed her lips and wiped her tears away gently with his dirty and calloused thumbs. Caleb and Carrie stood and watched silently, hardly daring to move, they didn't want to break the moment. Don suddenly realised what he had done and bustled away, looking embarrassed, and dropping poor Jane like she was scalding hot. Carrie moved next to Jane and gave her a hug. She whispered in her ear, "Be patient, he's come so far, we are rooting for you both." Jane just hugged her back, hiding a grin.

Caleb chatted to Don about the ponies, as if nothing had happened, and everyone relaxed with their tea. Juan appeared a few minutes later for his afternoon break and they all chatted about their day. Caleb sat and watched his team with silent awe. He was so proud of all of them, and very much in love with one of them, she was his world. He was a lucky man, his dream was coming together.

Chapter 15

Abandoning

The next morning, Carrie walked down to the farm gate to fetch the post. Just as she was turning away from the mailbox, she noticed a big, strong cardboard box tucked in the hedge by the gate. She opened the gate, cursing that a delivery had been left there, rather than being brought to the yard. As she bent to look at the label, the box seemed to wobble and she heard a low growl. This was no ordinary delivery. She carefully unstuck a corner of the box, which was taped shut, and peered inside. A very sharp set of teeth were bared at her through the gap and another, harsher growl came from within. "It's OK sweet one." she cooed, closing the gap and reaching for her phone.

Within minutes their 4x4 was heading towards her with Caleb and Jane inside. She showed them the box, which was now growling fiercely at the world. "I think we need to carry it as it is, we don't want the contents bursting out until we are inside somewhere!" Caleb and Carrie carefully lifted the box into the back of the 4x4. The grumbling and growling didn't stop all the way to the veterinary building. Jane had gone ahead, on foot, to open up and prepare a pen for the monster in the box.

They carefully carried the box in and set it down in a big pen. Jane had thrown in a comfy dog bed and filled a water bowl. All three stood for a moment and discussed how to let the poor dog out, without getting eaten alive. Jane suggested gauntlets, but then realised they wouldn't be able to take the tape off the box with them on. They thought about cutting the tape with a sharp knife and then watched the box wobbling around as the dog tried to get out and decided a knife was too much of a risk, either they, or the dog, would get hurt. "I wonder what's in there, it sounds like a Dobermann or something, but the box isn't big enough for that." Carrie laughed.

"Whatever it is it wants out, and wants us for breakfast." giggled Jane. Caleb manfully insisted that the ladies stand back, shut the door of the pen behind him and began peeling off the tape holding the box shut. All was quiet at first, as the dog considered its options, then the growling started again. With just one piece of tape left to remove Caleb stood back and prepared himself. "Be careful," warned Carrie unnecessarily. He pulled the last long piece of tape upwards and off the lid of the box, as he stepped away quickly. The flaps of the box opened, as he pulled, and the cutest little Jack Russell type head shot through the gap. It looked around, saw Caleb, and jumped out of the box towards him. Caleb backed against the wall and said, "Hey sweet one." in what was meant to be a soothing voice. It came out as more of an incoherent squeak! The dog stood and regarded him for a couple of seconds then bounded at him, wagging its tail and making sweet little whines to be stroked. Caleb crouched down and let the little dog sniff his hand. It immediately lay down and offered its huge tummy for a rub, still wagging its tail. Everyone drew a huge breath and burst out laughing.

Jane came into the pen to examine the huge belly and see what was going on. The dog, or bitch, as she pointed out, was in good condition, apart from its enormous tummy. On quick inspection, she confirmed what they all guessed, she was full of pups and ready to give birth. On closer examination, she grew concerned. "Either there is a huge litter of pups in here or she has been mated with a much bigger dog. I suspect the latter. I'm going to get scrubbed up and have an internal feel. Carrie can you find the ultrasound equipment and we'll try that too. She looks like she may have been in labour a while but nothing is showing, I may have to do a caesarean on her, urgently. Caleb can you take her to a surgery room?"

Carrie found the box with the new ultrasound probe and monitor in it and hastily unpacked it. She carried it to Jane, who was examining the poor dog internally with a well lubed finger. Jane gave her and Caleb instructions on how to set it up, while she palpated and prodded. So far, the little dog was putting up with it but she was beginning to look stressed again. Thankfully the ultrasound came on with a little hum when they flipped the switch. The dog's belly was fairly free of hair so Jane slapped some gel on the probe and started looking. To Caleb and Carrie, the picture on the screen was a mystery, but Jane seemed to find out what she needed to know. "The pups are huge, way too big for her to push them out. I will have to go in and get them."

Jane told them what she needed. Her own stash of basic drugs were already in the prep room, thank goodness. She weighed the dog quickly and gently injected her with general anaesthetic. Carrie found her the right tubes and Jane intubated the dog and instructed Caleb how to watch her breathing, he was to shout if anything changed. Carrie found some towels and Jane cleaned the site where her cut would be made. Jane said. "If we had time, I would prefer a trained nurse here, but if we all keep calm and shout out any changes we see, we should be fine." Caleb watched the breathing like a hawk and Jane stepped away to scrub up again. She came back, asked if everything looked good, had a last listen to the little dog's heart and made her incision. Carrie watched in awe as Jane cut down through the skin and into the lower layers. Suddenly she popped her hand into the incision and gently pulled a smooth lump to the surface. "First pup coming out, how's the breathing?"

"She looks just the same and the balloon thingy is going in and out," said Caleb.

Jane made a little hole, in what Carrie assumed was the placenta, and pulled out a chubby length of slimy pup. Carrie grabbed it from her and started rubbing it with the towel to stimulate it to breathe. She checked it had no mucus around its nose and prayed for it to show some life. It felt alive, it wiggled slightly and gave a squeak as she rubbed it. Jane called out, "Leave it in the towel somewhere it can't roll and come and get the next one." Carrie did as she was told and soon had a second squirmy pup cuddled up with the first. Two more slightly smaller pups arrived and were squeaking away within just a few moments. Jane removed what she said was the last pup, but did not hand it to Carrie. Jane wiped it down and put her stethoscope to its chest, then shook her head sadly. "I think this one's been dead a few hours, he looks like the runt and I guess he wasn't strong enough to cope with all the upheaval. Poor little pup." There was no time to mourn, as Jane needed to stitch Mum up. Carrie watched the babies, to check they all stayed healthy. Soon enough, Mum was finished and laid in her new bed in the pen, to come round. Caleb sat watching her. The pups were all placed, huddled together, in another bed right beside Mum, gently wriggling and whining. Carrie came to sit with Caleb, as Jane went to clean up and get out of her scrubs. "Well," said Caleb, "that was some delivery, I must have words with the postman!" They both giggled as they watched Mum and pups sleeping.

Jane returned to the pen and sat beside the others with a sigh and a grin. "It feels good to be a vet again, how are they doing?"

"Mum had started to stir, but now she looks like she's asleep again. The pups all look fine, wiggly and cute, can you tell what sex they are?"

Jane knelt down and picked the pups up one at a time. She looked in their mouths and had a quick feel all over, then she looked at their undercarriage. "The little one that's nearly all brown, and the brown and white one are girls, the other two, with the black bits mixed in, are boys. They all look good and healthy."

"Aww, they look really pissed that you disturbed them," laughed Caleb, "they're all squirmy now, trying to get comfy again." The sounds they were making were deafening, for four such small pups.

As they watched, Mum slowly started to stir. She lay quite happily looking around and even wagged her tail when Caleb spoke to her. Within a few minutes she was conscious enough to hear her pups squeaking and she tried to stand. It took her a couple of goes to get to her feet, but she persisted and staggered over to the bed of pups. The three of them held their breath as she sniffed the pups and nuzzled the nearest one. She climbed into their bed, with wobbly legs, and carefully lay down next to them. They sensed her presence and all nuzzled into her belly. The two bigger pups found her teats straight away and began guzzling milk. Jane gently positioned the other two on teats and they sucked away as well. Mum lay there looking very content, licking the back of the nearest pup as it drank. "Wow, isn't instinct a wonderful thing, look how peaceful they all are," said Caleb, getting a bit misty eyed.

"You wait until they're a few weeks old and all pushing and shoving for milk, it's not so peaceful then," laughed Jane.

"Should we name them all, or wait?" asked Carrie. "We should try and find out who the mum belongs to, they might have just panicked and left her here hoping we would help. Maybe they want her back, or at least want to know she's OK. I feel mad that they just left her at the gate, but maybe they have no money for a vet or something. We could ask Julian or the shop lady if they recognise Mum."

"All those are good points, we need to talk about a policy for this sort of situation. Then we can tell everyone how to access our help safely if they are stuck. The little mum must be local, no one else really knows what we do yet, do they?" said Caleb.

"I think word will have spread pretty quickly since the bonfire party, but maybe she is local, we should ask around," said Jane. "Do they deserve her back though? She and her pups could have died in that box, if you hadn't collected the post until this afternoon. It doesn't bear thinking about really."

Mum and pups were left in peace for a short while, after a good meal for Mum. She was hungry and ate the whole bowl of food. Jane volunteered to check up on them through the day and Carrie and Caleb would check through the night. They all headed back to the barn for a break and to discuss what issues the morning's events had highlighted. Each of them was sure, it wouldn't be the last such delivery.

"OK, let's go round each of us and see what improvements we can make in light of what just happened. Jane, incredible vetting by the way, we all felt safe in your hands. Can you start, we were definitely not prepared surgery wise, which is my fault, not yours, what do we need to do most urgently?"

"I think I'd like to spend a few days in the veterinary building, unpacking and checking everything and listing any omissions, it's only when you use stuff, you realise what's been forgotten. Also, I need to be more familiar with the layout and the equipment so I don't have to waste time in an emergency. You two did an amazing job as vet nurses but, if this is going to happen again, I need someone who is trained to monitor anaesthetics and get me what I need, before I know I need it. I don't know how we can justify someone else though, if this remains a rare thing. When are you planning to ramp up the number of animals we have?"

"We were hoping we'd get married in August, before we really got going, animal wise. You spending time in the vet rooms is absolutely no problem, in fact, it means you can keep an eye on Mum and pups, so let's start that straight away. Carrie would you be happy helping Jane and learning a bit more, just in case another case comes in soon?"

"Yes, I was going to suggest it myself, I felt clueless in there! If Jane's happy to explain things as we work, I'll learn all I can. Should we start looking for a vet nurse today though? Or will I do for now?"

206

Jane laughed, "You'll do for now, I know you learn fast and think on your feet. If we have more than the odd case, can we think again though? I'd hate to lose a patient due to one of us making an error under pressure."

Caleb asked, "Do you know anyone who might want the job Jane? It'd be lovely to take on someone you already trust."

"There is one person, who would fit right in, but she has a job. Can I talk to her about the idea before I name her?"

"Of course you can," said Carrie. "If she's interested, we could offer her the same deal we offered you, general work until vet work is needed, but at vet nurse pay. If she's the right person it will be worth it, like it is with you." Carrie looked at Caleb for confirmation as she said this and he nodded his agreement.

"OK, so that sorts the vet bit, what are we going to do about avoiding midnight animal deliveries? How can we persuade people they can ask us to take their animals, they don't have to abandon them at the gate? I can fit CCTV, which will help us to spot boxes and maybe put people off a bit. I want us to get these animals to safety though, not put people off if they need our help."

"We need a big sign, first of all, explaining that we don't judge and that they only have to phone us and we will offer help to any animal. Could we put posters in the village too? We could have a dedicated phone and put the number on the sign. One of us can carry the phone at all times and answer the calls as they come in. If we have it constantly on voice-mail, in case we miss a call, they can leave a number and we can contact them. CCTV for definite too. We could pay for an advert on local radio or the local newspaper. We also need to make sure the police, social services, the vicars, the shops and local councils know they can call us anytime. They are the sort of people who might hear of owners struggling or an animal suffering. OK, that's me done, Caleb?"

"Wow Carrie, anyone would think you had been doing this for years, well thought out girl," said Jane.

Caleb hugged her. "You always have great solutions, I'd only got as far as a sign, you have covered everything! Thanks Sweetie."

Caleb jotted down all the ideas Carrie had, so none of them got forgot.

They explained the problem to Juan and Don when they appeared for their break. Juan, ever practical, suggested a leaflet drop around the village and posters further afield. Don thought a newspaper article or radio interview with Caleb would catch everyone's attention. "Why not cash in on your fame, no radio station or newspaper will turn you away. An advert costs big money but an interview with Caleb Kirkmichael will almost have them paying you!"

Carrie agreed with Don. "You said that your lawyer confirmed everything was in order with the council, the sanctuary can be up and running now. I think a round of interviews is a great idea. If we get really busy, we can keep the wedding small and save the honeymoon for another year. I don't mind how we get married as long as we do. Why not 'open for business' now, rather than waiting? Let's get all the publicity we can and save some animals."

Caleb turned to her and kissed her long and hard, to the accompaniment of groans from the team. "You are amazing Carrie, don't ever forget it. OK, so, plan for the next few days, Carrie and Jane in the vet building, sorting, learning and cooing over puppies. Me on the phone talking to anyone and everyone. Juan, can you take responsibility for anything that I might miss if I am stuck inside on the phone. Can the haymaking wait for a few more days, it looks like it might rain tomorrow anyway. You can come and find me if you need any decisions making. Can we make a list of the drugs you need Jane and tell me how to order them, I assume you have to take responsibility for them?"

Juan agreed that there was no point starting cutting hay for a few days, and was happy to keep his eye on everything else. Jane said she would find out what she had to do, to be allowed to order drugs, and would list what they needed. She also said she was going for a drink with the vet nurse she mentioned, that evening, and would report back tomorrow.

"Don, would you mind checking our remaining horses for us a couple of times a day for a few days? If Carrie and I are both so involved, it will be one thing less to think about. Also, as the horse's feet are fine at the minute, would you consider helping me and Juan to get the hay in once it's baled? I know it's heavy, dusty work but an extra pair of hands would be really useful, especially if I have to go and do these interviews at just the wrong moment or something."

"Of course I will, I was assuming I'd be needed, and you're paying me to work for you three days a week! I don't mind what I do, as long as you're happy with the arrangement. Is Monkey still OK out all day or is he getting fat? I am happy to bring him in each day if that helps?"

Carrie replied, "I think he needs to come in, I have been bringing him in on and off for a week or two. If you can handle the little darling, I would be glad to see him in every day."

"So, are we all happy?" Caleb asked. "If so, I'm going to cuddle some puppies for a while, then shut myself in the quarantine building and make calls in the peace and quiet. Anyone needing a puppy fix is welcome to join me." They all laughed and even Juan followed them down to the vet building, "Just in case I recognise the bitch."

When they went into the penned area, they heard a little yap and Mum came to the pen door to meet them. As the outer doors were shut, they let her out of the pen for a wander around. She greeted everyone with wagging tail and licks for any skin she could reach. Jane and Carrie went in to see the pups and check all was well. Their eyes would not open for a while yet but they were all contentedly wriggling in a big heap in the bed. Jane checked they were warm and Carrie asked, "Is it OK to pick them up? I need to snuggle."

We should probably let Mum see us touching them, rather than just taking one now. Let's get her back in here and see how she reacts. Caleb and the others came into the pen and Mum followed. They all knelt along the wall, away from the dog bed and Jane called Mum over to the pups. While Mum was watching her, she gently lifted a pup and snuggled it. Mum watched happily with her tail wagging. No problem there then. Jane handed the first pup to Carrie and lifted another, handing it to Caleb. Mum came over to sniff them both, as they held her pups, but seemed very relaxed. Jane took the last two and offered one each to Don and Juan. As they all knelt side by side with pups in their arms Mum just wagged and sniffed and watched happily. After a couple of minutes, Jane reversed the process and gently returned the pups to their bed. When they were all back everyone made a fuss of Mum and told her what a good girl she was. She took her praise happily and then returned to the pups and lay down for them to feed. "How could anyone just dump such a kind little dog, in a box, when she needed them most?" asked Juan as they trooped out of the pen, "The owners want shooting in my book, poor little mites."

"I can't believe it's the same dog we thought was going to eat us this morning," said Carrie, "she must have been so scared in that box, not knowing what was going on, and in pain, with her labour started. She was trying to protect herself and her pups by sounding tough and growling. As soon as Caleb opened the box and she saw he wasn't fierce or dangerous she became as friendly as she is now."

"Hey," said Caleb, "I am a bit fierce and dangerous, and tall, dark and handsome, all those adoring fans can't be wrong you know!"

Chapter 16

Vetting

Carrie and Jane planned to spend the next few days unpacking, sorting and learning about all the new equipment. Jane was like a kid in a candy shop as she opened boxes, explained items and found appropriate homes for them. All the smaller items were stored away carefully in the cabinets designed for them. The larger equipment was placed around the rooms in a plan that only Jane knew, it had been in her head for weeks. Whenever there was a gap in the proceedings, the women popped into Mum's cage and played with puppies. Mum was happily going outside for a few minutes' walk and a toilet break now. They took it in turns to walk Mum or play with the pups. During the warmest part of each day, they opened the pens outside run, so Mum could take herself out for a bit of fresh air between walks. The pups were more active now, clambering over each other and making lots of noise. Their eyes would not open until they were about fourteen days old, but that did not stop them wiggling around.

Jane had found out how to register the vet building as a Veterinary Practice Premises. She had filled in the forms, read all the requirements and was waiting for an inspection. She hoped everything was in order, they had temperature controlled storage, a locking fridge and locked cabinets for the Controlled Drugs. She even had a locking cabinet fixed in her car that had been there since her last job. She needed a register to record all the drugs that came in and out. She had ordered a hardbound record book from a veterinary supplier, as the record had to be permanent, not one where pages could be removed. Just to confuse, she had to prove she kept records of withdrawal periods too, relevant to using drugs on animals that may end up in the food chain. This included horses, even though there was no chance their horses would ever be food for anyone. All she could do now was wait for the inspectors and pray she had thought of everything.

Caleb had a good day on the phone. He found numbers for the local council and social services and asked to be added to their list of useful numbers, if they heard of animals needing assistance, especially in emergencies. He rang the local police headquarters and the emergency joint control centre with the same request. Both the local radio station and the local paper were falling over themselves to do interviews, once they were convinced who he was. The regional TV broadcasters were equally keen and wanted to come to the farm tomorrow.

Carrie and Caleb spent the evening wording a sign for the front gate, telling people the number to ring for help. The sign basically said they would take any animal for any reason and would not judge. It also stated that animals could be left anonymously just by ringing the number and arranging a drop off time. In big letters, it stated, 'FOR THE ANIMAL'S WELFARE, PLEASE DO NOT LEAVE THEM AT THE GATE WITHOUT LETTING US KNOW THEY ARE THERE'. Underneath it said that anyone struggling to care for a pet could ring for advice and practical or veterinary help at any time. They would use the same wording on posters for the villages. Caleb popped into town early next morning and took out a contract for a new mobile phone, to use for the emergency number. He added the new phone number to the design for the sign and took it to a sign maker. It would be ready and delivered that very day. Having a famous face definitely had its benefits. He then took another similar design, with the new number added, to a printer and ordered a hundred A4 posters.

When Caleb returned to the farm, he dropped into the vet building to see Carrie and Jane. Jane had just started telling Carrie about her evening with the vet nurse. She started again for Caleb's benefit.

"I actually ended up drinking with two vet nurses. At least, one who used to be a vet nurse and one who still is. I very cautiously started to ask questions about whether they're happy in their jobs. Big mistake. They work for Scarton practice and are both really fed up. They're committed animal people and don't want to change careers, but neither of them can stand the Senior Partner, the vet who ditched me. I think he's having a mid-life crisis or something, he's making everyone's life a misery. So, the long and the short is, they'd both like to leave, and either of them would fit our requirements. I decided not to tell them about there actually being a job here, I didn't want them fighting for it in front of me! The lady, who is no longer a vet nurse, is now the practice manager. The younger lad, who is currently a vet nurse, has been qualified for three years and is very good at his job. So, the more mature and very experienced lady is a great vet nurse and an awesome manager and administrator, but she is on a higher wage. The younger lad is a great vet nurse and, what he lacks in experience, he makes up for in sheer talent and passion. I would employ either, or both of them, if it was my practice. If I had to choose, that would be harder, but if money's no object then it'd be Jan, the practice manager. Her knowledge would put many vets to shame, she's highly qualified and very experienced. If she could be a vet nurse and manager of the vet building, you'd be getting good value for money. She's also a really nice person."

Carrie added, "She spoke to me the day the horses all arrived, I remember being impressed by her then. She didn't know us at all, yet she fitted us in, the same day, and made me feel that we mattered to her. She had a great manner, despite the fact that I probably put her on the spot, and best of all, she sent you to us Jane!"

"Well, I'm convinced," said Caleb, "we just need to research how much she is likely to cost us, and whether we can rescue the young lad as well. It **is** what we do, after all! What's his name by the way?"

"He's Josh, and he's in his mid-twenties. I can tell you roughly what they earn as I asked them for a ballpark figure, just in conversation, saying I'd look out for jobs for them." Jane told them the figures.

Carrie nodded and Caleb smiled. "It's a good job we don't have to rely on donations, but I always told myself I'd have the best team I could, and that costs money. Let's arrange interviews and see how keen they are, they'll both have to be willing to work where they are needed and muck in with anything. Shall I approach them or would you like to Jane? I think they should report to you, if they work here, so I'm happy for you to do it. I'm sure Carrie and I will want to be at the interviews though, as we're paying the wages."

Jane replied, "I'd love to tell them they have interviews, I hope they'll both be over the moon. Will you accept my word for their good character, as a reference, just in case their boss refuses. He'll panic if he thinks he's losing two more staff, he'll probably make their life hell while he can."

"If they seem right at the interview, we'll be happy to take them, reference or not. We didn't ask for a reference for you, we knew it'd be biased as hell. He needn't know where they are going until they leave, if that's what they want."

Jane smiled, and started a group hug, "Thanks guys, they are such good people, and my friends, they stood up for me, when everyone else there was sucking up to the boss. I'll be so excited to offer them interviews. Can I call them now?"

Carrie laughed. "Won't that be a bit obvious, if they're at work today?"

"I'm nothing if not resourceful, I'll be discreet. When should they come?"

"Do you think they'd come tonight, after work? The TV people are coming this afternoon but they'll be gone by 5pm. It would be great to get it settled."

"Leave it with me, I'll see what they say."

Jane shot off into another room to ring Jan and Josh. Meanwhile, a call on Caleb's mobile told him the sign was being delivered and did he want them to fix it to the gate for him. He rushed out to thank them in person and Carrie went to visit Mum and her pups.

Ten minutes later and Jane was back, only Carrie and Caleb had disappeared. Jane was surprised, then it dawned on her – puppies! Sure enough, she found Carrie with Mum on her lap and Caleb snuggling a pup or two. "How did I guess this is where I'd find you?" She grinned.

"Never mind that, how did you get on?"

"Well, Jan was in her office and able to talk freely. She was, cautiously, very excited to come and see us and talk. I forgot that Josh is not allowed his mobile when he's working, so I couldn't talk to him directly. I told Jan all I could and explained we would like to interview both her and Josh for a position each. She is going to call him into her office and quietly tell him. I said he could ring me in his lunch break with any questions and that we'd like them both to come here at 5.30pm today."

"Brilliant, well done. Let's hope they are both keen when they meet us. Shall we break for lunch now? We need to prepare for the TV crew Carrie, and I'm starving. Are you OK to be on TV Jane, when we look around in here? I hope we can show Mum and the pups, they'll have even more adoring fans than I've got!" said Caleb.

"Mum's a natural and the pups won't even know

anything's happening, and yes I'm OK with being on TV, if it helps the cause, should I find a white lab coat and wear my stethoscope?" Jane giggled.

The three of them walked up towards the barn for lunch, discussing which bits of the farm the TV crew would want to film. Caleb told them the new sign was delivered and erected already. They promised to go and see it later. Don had bought Monkey into the courtyard so Carrie went and gave him a quick brush to make him presentable – he was another natural for filming. Caleb heated some soup for them as Jane tucked into her sandwich. Juan appeared moments later and Jane rang Don to see where he was. When they were all settled and eating, talk of the afternoons filming carried on. Juan and Don were keen to stay out of sight but Caleb wanted to show Don's forge in action – the sparks, as Don hammered hot metal, would make a good show. Don agreed as long as he didn't have to speak.

When the TV crew arrived at 2pm Carrie and Caleb were there to meet them. Being local TV, the presenter was a bit awestruck by Caleb, it's not every day he got to interview big stars. Caleb was the master of putting people at ease, very soon everyone was laughing and relaxed. They started with the big signs at the gate with Caleb explaining the role of the sanctuary and explaining about Mum and the puppies, and why people should feel safe to ask for help. Then they went to the vet building and the quarantine area to show the facilities. Jane was a star, explaining how much they could do for animals there. The visit to Mum and pups was a huge success, with Mum trying to lick the camera to death and the pups squirming cutely to order. Caleb reiterated why animals should not be left at the gate and Jane explained that Mum and pups could have died if they hadn't found them early. Don's forge was next and, as requested, he worked a hot horseshoe on his anvil, with sparks flying. Then they headed to the courtyard and filmed Monkey, who also tried to eat the camera. Carrie explained why he was in his pen and how he, and the others, came to be at the sanctuary. Finally, Caleb explained about their policy of re-homing animals and the success story of the horses having new homes now.

When they had all the shots they needed, the film crew and presenter joined the team for a late afternoon break in the barn. Carrie explained Winnie and why they were living in a barn. The presenter made the camera guy get some shots of Winnie and them having tea as an extra story to add. Juan tried to hide but he ended up having his few moments of fame in the end.

After the crew had gone, they all sat discussing the experience. Caleb had been totally at ease, of course, but the others had found it a bit daunting. "You never think about how you sound, or look, but I found myself worrying about it today," said Jane.

"I know, I felt like a fraud hammering that shoe, but I guess it will look real to people watching."

Carrie added, "Talking to a camera is really hard, you feel so exposed. Monkey was really camera shy, he only ate a bit of it! He got a better mouthful of the boom mike, or whatever it's called, the big, furry, sound thing. The poor sound guy had to wrestle it out of his mouth. I'm not sure it worked so well when it was covered in horse spit."

"Mum dog tried that too, she licked the lens twice and they had to stop and clean it. She was a star though. Hopefully, we got all the messages across we needed to. I can't wait to see the end result." Caleb looked really excited, for someone who spent half his life being filmed.

"Do we get to see it before it goes out?" asked Carrie.

"I'm afraid I used my stern voice and insisted, I waffled about needing to protect my image and stuff. They agreed to show us first," answered Caleb.

Suddenly Carrie looked at her watch. "We only have an hour before Jane's friends arrive for interviews, we'd better get organised."

Don and Juan headed home for the day and the others discussed a plan of action for the interviews. They decided they should show Jan and Josh around together, then have a chat with them separately to explain wages and duties. Carrie was keen for the interviews to feel informal, so there was no script of questions or planning. She felt they would learn more about Josh and Jan's personalities if they were relaxed and informal. By the time they both arrived the kettle was on, they decided an informal start was a good excuse for another drink.

"Hi Jan, Josh, good to meet you," Caleb called as they got out of the car. "Come and sit, tea or coffee?"

Carrie continued, "Thanks for coming at such

225

short notice, we're keen to get our staffing levels right, now our new buildings are ready to go. I'm sure Jane has told you the basics of what we want. In the long run, we would like you, Jan, to manage the veterinary and quarantine centres, working with Jane and reporting to her, standing in as head vet nurse when necessary. Josh, we need your skills as a vet nurse and animal care manager when the centres are fully up and running. We may need more help as the centres grow and, if we do, we see Josh becoming head nurse and Jan overseeing any other staff as part of her role. Those are the plans, but we need you both to be flexible and be prepared to do whatever is needed to care for the animals. At first, there will be very little animal work, as we currently only have one dog and her pups in the centre. Until it builds up, we would need you to do whatever jobs you are asked to do, or whatever jobs you think need doing. We aim to build a team of friends around us to run the place, with everyone having a main role, but everyone pitching in when needed for any other jobs. So far, we have three staff and Caleb and I are also very much part of the team. We have Juan who is farm manager, caring for the outside spaces and land. We have Don who is our farrier, working for us three days a week and himself the other days. Of course, we also have Jane who is our head, and only,

Veterinary Surgeon. We live on site, in Winnie here at the moment," she said, pointing to the motor home. "Everyone else is local, by choice, as we all know animal care can be needed twenty-four hours a day. We'd need you to be prepared to respond to urgent situations, out of hours, and maybe take shifts if an animal needed night time care. Any such overtime will be paid. Any questions?"

Caleb had been watching her with pride as she spoke. "I think Carrie has covered nearly everything. Let's chat, while we finish our drinks, then we'll do the grand tour."

They visited the horses in the fields and Monkey in the yard. Caleb explained that they hoped the horses would be the main part of their rescue work and asked whether either of them were used to handling horses. Jan was a regular rider and had worked with horses after she first qualified. Josh was not a horse person but had grown up on a dairy farm, so their size didn't worry him, and he was keen to learn. He said he'd handled calves bigger than Monkey! As usual, Monkey stole the show, stretching his head up and pulling faces when Jan gave him a back scratch. Caleb had to drag the group away from the little man to continue the tour. When they

227

entered the vet centre, both Jan and Josh were really excited. "Wow, so much space, so much new stuff. Who designed the layout, it's perfect?" asked Jan. Jane looked embarrassed as Caleb gave her a pat on the back.

"Mostly Jane's doing. We all had a little hand in it, but Jane was the one with the knowledge and ideas."

Josh was opening drawers and looking in cupboards in awe. Suddenly he realised that might be a bit rude. "I'm so sorry, I got carried away imagining working here, it's wonderful. Do you have an X-ray room? Where do you treat horses? Where are the small animals going to live? I have sooo many questions!"

Carrie laughed. "Look anywhere you like and enjoy it while it's still pristine, very soon I hope everything will look a bit more used. Yes, we have an X-ray machine and there is a big area out the back for horses or big animals. As for the small animal accommodation, come this way."

They trooped out to the area behind the vet rooms. As soon as the door opened, Mum was at her pen door whining and wagging a greeting. As Josh and Jan admired the pens and cages, Carrie let her out for a sniff at the visitors. She charged around not knowing who to greet first. Jan stooped to chat to her and she was straight on her back for a belly rub. Jan saw the scar and asked, "What's this little love's story then?"

Carrie told the story of finding her in a box by the gate, already in labour. She showed Jan the puppies and explained their measures to ensure no other animal was put at risk like that. Jan said, "I remember when I first started at Scarton, there was a spate of that, I think a local factory had shut and many locals were on the dole suddenly. It was so sad, they all got sent to a rescue place miles away. Now we have one on our doorstep."

"OK, let's have a quick look at the quarantine centre next door, then we'll have a word with each of you individually and talk business. I assume you are both interested in learning more?" Caleb didn't want to take anything for granted.

They both nodded to Caleb's question and followed them to the quarantine building. While they looked around with Caleb, Carrie and Jane had a quiet chat. "They both seem really lovely, well done

Jane. Do you think they will accept jobs?"

"I am sure they'll both be very tempted, time will tell. How shall we do the next bit, it seems strange to leave one sitting outside alone while the rest of us interview the other?"

"Why don't I sit out here with one, while you and Caleb interview the other. I already like them both, I feel I might learn more, with an informal chat, than I would sitting in on the interview. The only thing I ask is that we have a month's trial, I'd hate to find out too late if they don't fit in. It seems unlikely though, they're both good people, as you told us. I'll tell Caleb my plan and we'll go from there."

Caleb and the interviewees returned, Carrie took him to one side and explained what she and Jane discussed. He was very happy with the idea and the interviews commenced. Carrie had Josh first and they chatted away about all sorts. She knew he grew up on a farm so they talked farming for a bit. He had two sisters and his parents still farmed locally. He was single and happy that way at present. Carrie talked about her life and how she met Caleb. She explained that this place was his long-term dream. He asked questions about funding and job security.

Carrie laughed awkwardly and explained that Caleb had just sold his house in Hollywood for six times what the farm, new buildings and equipment had cost. His earnings over the years meant he was quite able to offer job security for decades to come. Josh wanted to talk about Caleb and his films then, so they did.

Jan came out of the interview smiling and gave Josh a high five as he went in. Carrie sat with Jan and asked her how she was feeling about the job. Jan laughed. "What's not to like? I would be extremely tempted, even if I wasn't so unhappy in my current job. With that added pressure I've already told Jane and Caleb I'm in, if you'll have me!"

Carrie gave her a hug, "Welcome to our team, I'm so pleased. Jane was full of praise for you and, from what I've seen today, it was well deserved. Are you happy with mucking in with menial jobs for now, until we get busy?"

"Of course, it will make a nice break from the stress, although I'll be glad to get back to managing when the time comes. The only thing that worried me a bit, is how you are funded. Are you opening the practice to the public, or do you have to fundraise?"

Carrie laughed again, "I had the same question from Josh, you are both sensible people. Caleb has had a very successful career in films, as I'm sure you realise. Over the years he has also had some very good investment advice. Suffice to say, the money is never likely to run short, and if it ever does, he can do another film, and earn more than you or I could in a lifetime, for a couple of months work. It's crazy, but it's the truth. I've seen the bank accounts, I'm a signatory on most of them. You'll never have to wait for your wages and never have to bag pack in Tesco's to feed the animals in your care. I hope that puts your mind at rest, but please, keep it to yourself."

"Wow, I never thought that through, I mean, I guessed he was rich, but, to spend it all on something like this is.......incredible, and cool! I feel better for knowing he is a good guy, not a.........well, he's a good guy!"

"Not an entitled, rich git," Carrie laughed as she guessed what Jan was going to say. "He's definitely a good guy, and this has been his dream for years, it's not just a whim of his. I know I'm biased, being his fiancée, but he's the kindest and most thoughtful person. Your job security here will be as good as anywhere, better than most places. As long as you're a team player we'll be happy."

"Thanks for explaining, and sorry I nearly said something rude! I am doubly glad I followed my instincts and accepted now."

As they chatted on, Carrie became more and more sure that Jan was a good choice. Carrie told her she had a crash course in vet nursing with Mum's urgent caesarean, and was secretly glad she didn't need to do it anymore. "I can learn at my own pace from you, Josh and Jane now, and leave the room when it gets too icky! I might come in for the next birth though, that bit was amazing."

Jan laughed, "Everyone loves a birth, there'll be a queue."

Just then, Josh, Jane and Caleb came out of their interview. Josh looked at Jan and said, "Can I have a word in private Jan?" Caleb showed them back into the interview room and left them to chat. Carrie raised an eyebrow to Caleb, silently asking what had gone on. He shook his head as if to say he didn't know. After a few minutes Jan and a slightly tearful looking Josh came out. Caleb jumped in, saying, "Let's put the kettle on, back at the barn, and you can tell us what's worrying you, Josh. I don't expect it's anything we can't fix." They headed back to the barn, Jan with her arm around Josh as they walked. Carrie was concerned, but kept her silence until they all had a drink in hand.

She took the lead in breaking the silence. "What's troubling you Josh, is it not the job for you? We won't be offended if you turn it down."

Josh whispered his reply, "I love this place and the job is wonderful, but I don't deserve it. I've done stuff, in the past, that I need to tell you about. Once I do, you probably won't want me." He started crying again.

Caleb reached over and squeezed his hand. "Was this misdemeanour while you were in your teens?"

"Yes."

"Is it something you would do now?"

"No, definitely not!"

"Did you get punished at the time?"

234

"Yes."

"Have you learnt from that experience?"

"Oh, God, yes. I caused so much hurt to my parents, never again!"

"Then you're just the person we want, and you don't even need to tell us what happened. I had a playboy lifestyle for years, money, drink, sex. Plus adoring women chucking themselves at me, wherever I was. I eventually grew up and realised what a prick I'd been. I was ashamed too. A kind and beautiful woman made me realise, those experiences made me what I am today. I can't change what I did, but I can be a better me now. If you have learnt, and want to be a better Josh, then we're good to go. It's up to you, but we still want you."

Still crying Josh said, "Can I accept the job please, and thank you for believing in me."

Caleb looked at Carrie and she blew him a kiss and winked. Jan hugged Josh and Jane chatted on excitedly about all the plans she had for them. As they left, Jan said, "Thank you for offering us both a great future, we won't let you down."

After they had gone Carrie hugged Caleb extra hard and said, "Thank you."

"For saying you are kind and beautiful? It's the truth."

"That too, but mainly for being the most empathetic and wonderful man in the world and giving that lad a chance. He won't let you down now, he was looking at you with even more hero worship after your 'prick' speech! It was inspired."

"It's a speech I didn't expect to make again, after I made it to you all those months ago, but it seemed appropriate. We all have a past."

"We do, but not everyone would admit it. Well done you, and well done Josh, he would have told you what it was he did I'm sure. Giving him the respect of allowing him to accept the job without telling us was genius. Real self-confidence building stuff. I love you more every day."

"Can I take you inside so you can prove it to me?" asked Caleb, wiggling his eyebrows in a very unsexy way.

236

Jane who had been sitting quietly watching them burst out laughing. "Hello, still here, I'm going now though, I don't want to cramp your style." She walked off down the drive, still giggling to herself.

Chapter 17

Searching

Carrie and Caleb lay in each other's arms, in bed, chatting about the day. Caleb was in no doubt, Carrie loved him more each day, and they were very relaxed. "What happened in the interviews then?" asked Carrie. "Did I miss any important bits?"

"Well, we talked about various things, but mainly pay and hours, stuff you already know. Jan was absolutely dead keen to take the job, she was very impressed with the vet centre. She loved the idea of managing and vet nursing, she likes variety. I think she'll be itching to get her teeth into the organising of both buildings. She says she loves record-keeping and admin. Strange woman! I think Jane was glad to hear she wasn't going to have to do it all. We need to think about who has the emergency phone, Jan would be very good with people, but I wondered if one of us should have it, what do you think?"

"Why don't we try making it one of Jan's responsibilities at first and see how it goes? She has the knowledge to answer questions that we don't in an emergency. Eventually, we'll want a receptionist and they can redirect calls to whoever is free, but that's probably a long way ahead."

"Good thinking. Both Jan and Josh have to give a month's notice, by the way. Jan thinks she's owed some leave, so she might escape earlier if she can. They're both going to hand in their notice first thing in the morning. Did you look at the sign while we were filming?"

"I did, it's good. Where is the emergency phone now?"

Caleb looked sheepish, "I think I left it in the vet centre. I'll go and get it. Let's hope there aren't any messages."

Early the next morning they had three surprise guests, at the gate, reading the sign. Carrie and Jane saw them as they made their way to the vet centre. Standing talking to one another were two men with a large lurcher type dog on a rope. Carrie went to greet them and see if she could help. The men called,

"Hello," as she approached. "We found this dog runnin' round with our cows this mornin', just up the road here, he weren't doin' any 'arm, but he can't stay there. I reckon he's a lampers dog, what's got lost. Can you take him?" Carrie opened the gate and crouched to greet the lurcher. He was hugely tall and skinny, although not really undernourished, just fit. She checked there was nothing to identify an owner on his collar. "Yes of course, we'll take him. Thanks for caring enough to bring him here. If you ever find any other animals just ring us and we'll come and get them. Do you want us to let you know if we find his owner or anything?"

"Nah, like I say it's likely some travellers dog. Not his fault mind, seems like a friendly big chap. We'll just leave him with you. Thanks." The farmworkers walked away, their duty done.

Carrie led the dog in and shut the gate. "Well fella, you're a fine big chap, come on, let's get you checked out." Jane had opened up the vet centre, while Carrie talked to the men and was waiting to welcome the lurcher.

"Hi, Lanky, what's your story then?" Jane ran her hands over the dog gently, checking for injury. "He

240

looks pretty healthy, did the men not want him or something?"

"They said they found him following their cows around the field. They thought he probably belonged to a lamper or travellers or something. They just wanted rid of him from near their livestock. At least they brought him here, instead of just chasing him away or shooting him. Do you think it's worth trying to find his owners?"

"Let's check him for a microchip first, just in case." Jane found the reader and ran it over the dog, nothing registered. "Oh well, it was worth a try. Let me check him over a bit more thoroughly, then he can go in a pen with some food and water, he's probably starving if he's been lost a while."

Carrie prepared a pen with a bed, a bowl of water and some food. Jane brought the dog through from the consulting room. "He seems fine, his coat is a bit tangled and he's grubby but otherwise he's good."

"OK, let's leave him here to settle and I'll ring around a few places to see if I can find his owners." Carrie headed for a phone, then realised she had no idea who to call. She started with the local police station but they had no reports of a lost dog. She tried the RSPCA, but they had no local centre and couldn't do more than take the dogs description, just in case someone reported it missing. This needed more thought. They needed a way of telling people about lost and found dogs. She suddenly thought, Social media! We should be tweeting or Facebooking to look for owners. Who's good at that stuff? We don't know any young people! It hit her within seconds – Josh. I wonder if he's a social media geek? "Jane," she called.

Jane appeared from the back rooms. "Jane do you know if Josh is into social media stuff?"

"Yes, that's why he wasn't allowed his phone when he was working, he got caught on it a couple of times and the boss banned him. He wasn't always on it, he just got caught in the act."

"Don't worry, it's a good thing for what I want here. I want to have a Facebook page for any lost pets we get. We need to spread the word on other people's pet based Facebook groups too. Maybe he'll know how to do all that. I can try and do it for now but I'm clueless."

Carrie signed into her Facebook account, which she hadn't used for months. She wondered how to find local pet groups. She didn't really know how to start. After a few minutes of fruitless searching she gave up. "I need help, I could waste hours here and get nowhere."

Carrie wandered up to Winnie, to look for Caleb. He was spending the morning on the phone and internet again, sorting out some stuff with his personal assistant, Lynne. She was the only member of staff he had left in the US. She dealt with all the correspondence still coming in from fans and various other sources. She also kept his own website up to date. He'd decided to post pictures of the sanctuary on there, to let his fans know what he was doing. Carrie found him typing an email to Lynne about the farm. He sat back when she appeared at the door of the motor home. "Hi lovely, do you need me?"

"Actually, I think I might need Lynne." She explained what she was trying to do and that she was failing miserably. "I know she was complaining she doesn't have much to do anymore, with you not filming and stuff. I wondered if she could take on setting up a website and a Facebook page for the farm, so we can let people know about lost dogs and

243

animals looking for homes. Oh, and by the way, we've gained another resident this morning, hence my need to get this sorted. We had a lost dog handed in at the gate."

"Great idea about a website and I'll get on to it with Lynne straight away. We might need some local knowledge to find Facebook pages to link to. First, I want to meet the new resident though, shall we go?"

They both made their way back to the vet centre and into the pens. Jane was still moving stuff around and planning, she just gave them a vague wave as they passed. Mum was at the door of her pen, whining and waiting for a fuss. In the next pen, a hairy head appeared, to see what all the noise was. Caleb said, "My he's big, he would tower over Mum, is he friendly?" Carrie nodded and opened the pen door. 'Lanky,' as she was already calling him in her head, just stood there wagging his tail and looking sleepy. Caleb put his hand out for sniffing and Lanky shuffled forward and lazily placed his head under the hand, asking for a stroke. His lolling tongue and dopey eyes made him look like anything but a sharp hunting dog. Once he'd had his petting from Caleb, he ambled away and lay back in his bed, staring into space happily. "He has to be the most chilled dog I've ever seen," laughed Caleb. They spent a few minutes with Mum and the pups then took Mum outside for a little walk. "Right, I'm going back to Winnie to ask Lynne about a website and Facebook page for us, what's your plan?" asked Caleb.

"I'm going to drag Jane away from her tidying and we'll go for a ride on Jaffa and Bilbo, she deserves a break and they need exercising. Unless you want to come instead?"

"No, one of us better slog away at the office work, while you're out enjoying yourself." he joked, as he dodged a playful slap.

Within twenty minutes they had the horses in and groomed and were tacking them up. Jane hadn't taken much persuading to leave her tidying and they were planning to head to the beach. Both horses were keen to go and the walk along the road to the slip-way only took ten minutes, they were soon walking along the wet sand. Carrie turned to Jane and asked, "How are things with you and Don. He seems so much happier, do you think he's ready for a new relationship yet?"

"We're still just friends, I don't think he can take

that last step yet. I'm sure he likes me, there have been definite flashes of chemistry and deeper feelings, but I'm scared to push. I know you've experienced grief like that, did it take a long time?"

"Yes ages, but some of that was me hanging onto the grief, like a safety blanket. If I was grieving, I couldn't move on with life. It was a cycle I stayed in far too long. Don is in that cycle too, I recognise the signs, he needs to take the risk and move on totally. Working for us is a huge start, but getting together with you will be the final step, and a very scary one. He wants to, I see it too, but he might need gentle pushes from his friends to give him courage. You may have to be patient a bit longer, but I'm sure he'll be worth the wait."

"Yes, I think he will, I can be patient. I love him already, but I can't tell him, that's hard."

"Talk to Caleb about how that feels, he waited months for me. I'm sure he'll have some words of support."

"Thanks, I might do that."

The tide was out and there were acres of smooth

wet sand stretching out before them. Carrie suggested they have a gallop, as the sand looked so inviting. Carrie and Jane urged the horses on and they were soon galloping fast, with the wind roaring in their ears. They started side by side but Bilbo was definitely feeling like a racehorse, he forged ahead with his ears pricked and his legs stretching out into a lovely powerful pace. He was enjoying it as much as Carrie and didn't need any urging now. They must have covered nearly a mile before either horse showed signs of slowing. They pulled up gradually, then walked along letting the horses catch their breath and cool down. It was a gorgeous day with the sun shining. Jane couldn't think of anywhere she'd rather be. The horses were relaxed after their gallop, they wandered along the water's edge paddling, as the sea ebbed and flowed under their feet. "I can't believe how lucky we are to be able to do this, in the middle of a working day. Thank you so much for giving me this opportunity, to work in a great place and be able to sneak off for a ride without any guilt – talk about perfect." Jane grinned at Carrie.

"You're welcome, and thank you for helping us make our dream come true. I still have to pinch myself when I see all we've achieved and how wonderful it is."

Just as they were thinking of turning back for home, they saw two people in the distance walking on the sand towards them. Carrie didn't think much of it at first, plenty of people walked on the beaches. As they neared the couple Carrie could see they were waving their arms at them, as if they wanted to flag them down. As they trotted over towards them, Carrie saw they were carrying a dog lead, and she began to wonder.

The man said, "Hi there, have you seen a loose dog? I lost him when we were out for a walk at 6am and haven't seen him since. He's a tall, thin, grey lurcher cross and very friendly."

Carrie smiled, happy to be able to put their minds at rest. "Yes, we have him, he's safe. We come from the new animal sanctuary at Cliff Top Farm, he was handed in by some farmers this morning. He's fine, you must have been worried sick!"

"Oh, thank goodness he's safe. We've been beside ourselves with worry. To be honest he's a bit of a dope. He never strays, but something must have spooked him, or smelt too good to miss, I just turned around and he was gone. We've been walking the beach and the cliffs for hours. Can we follow you there? We're desperate to see him."

"We're miles from the farm, do you have a car?"

"Yes, it's back in the town, we've walked miles too. Oh, I'm so relieved he's OK, I can't think straight!" said the lady.

Jane had a solution. "Why don't you walk with us, back to the slipway where we came down onto the beach. That's probably the nearest way back up anyway. If you wait there, we can ring for someone from the farm to come and fetch you and take you to him, what's his name by the way?"

"Wow, would you do that?" asked the lady. "It's so kind of you. Now I'm not so stressed, I feel totally exhausted. His name is Tiny, I think his first owner had a sense of humour. We re-homed him when he was eight months old and we love him to bits." They made their way back towards the slipway as they chatted.

Jane and Carrie laughed at the name. "We discovered he didn't have a microchip, which you should get done, by the way. I suppose I should ask you if he has any identifying marks, so we're sure you are his rightful owners, but I think you've told us enough for us to be pretty sure. I expect his reaction, when he sees you, will be telling enough anyway."

"To be honest I'm glad you did ask, it gives me confidence that he's with sensible people. He has a lumpy scar on his belly. He had surgery to remove a stone he swallowed, it was blocking his intestines. The vets X-rayed him and found it. Then he chewed his stitches out and had to be patched up a second time, it left quite a scar when it finally healed."

Jane had been listening to this and said, "I had wondered why the scar was so rough, I think you've proved he's yours. I'm the vet for the sanctuary, by the way, and I examined him when he came in."

"Wow, we didn't know you existed, you even have your own vet, why haven't we heard of you before?"

Carrie went on to explain all about the new sanctuary and what they were planning. She told them about Mum and pups and the horses and the new buildings, they were really interested.

"Can we make a donation, as a thank you for keeping Tiny safe? You must have to fundraise constantly to run all of that."

Carrie then had to explain that they were not that sort of charity, that the funds were from a private source and not donations. That bit always made her uncomfortable.

Jane made a brilliant suggestion, as usual. "The one thing we're trying to improve at present is our publicity. We have all those facilities and not many animals yet. If you'd like to help us, maybe you could give us a little of your time to help with leaflet drops or putting up posters around town. The more people who know we're here the better."

"That's a great idea, we could do that while we're walking Tiny, he's never going off the lead again." They both laughed.

The distance, that had taken the horses moments to gallop, now took ages to walk, but they were getting there. Suddenly the lady tripped badly on some seaweed and fell. Her partner, laughing at her misfortune, leaned over to give her a pull up. As she stood, she cried out and sat down again, hard.

"Oww, my ankle, I think I've twisted it, what an idiot, I'm not sure I can walk for a minute." Her partner sat beside her and hugged her. "Sorry darling, I didn't mean to hurt you, or laugh. You did look a bit funny though, sprawling on the wet sand!" She laughed too.

Jane dismounted from Jaffa and handed his reins to Carrie. "Let me have a quick look, just in case it's broken." She rolled up the lady's trouser leg and gently felt her ankle. "It looks like just a sprain, but you should keep off it until you get it checked out. How are we going to get you off the beach? I'll try my phone but it doesn't usually work down here, no signal."

Jane, Carrie and the man all tried their phones, but no one had any luck. Carrie suggested, "If you and your wife wait here, we'll ride up higher, where the signal is better and phone for someone to come and get you. Just be patient, we will get help."

With thanks and apologies, the couple waved the horses off. Carrie and Jane cantered back to the slipway and trotted up to the top of the cliffs. Jane's phone picked up a signal and she phoned Don. Once she'd explained what they needed they started the ride home. In a short while the farm's 4x4 appeared, heading down the road towards them. Caleb stopped and leant out of the window to ask for directions to the casualty. Don was sat beside him and called out. "Never a dull moment here, sounds like you've rescued some more waifs and strays Carrie!"

She laughed. "Make sure you bring them to the farm, you won't believe it, but they're the owners of the lurcher handed in this morning. I don't think her injury is bad, and they're desperate to see the dog."

Caleb let out the clutch and gently headed away from the horses, speeding up more than he really needed to once he was a little distance away. "Looks like they think they're on Bay Watch, rushing to the aid of a pretty girl in a bikini." Laughed Carrie.

"I think they'll be disappointed when they find her in a sensible coat and walking boots, with a husband in tow!" Jane giggled.

"I hope they don't go mad and get the jeep stuck in the sand, that would be very embarrassing." They laughed most of the way home. Jane brushed the horses down and put them back in their field, while Carrie put the kettle on and went to fetch Tiny. She let Mum out for a few seconds and found a lead for the lurcher. As she led him up the drive, towards the barn, she heard the 4x4 turning in the gate. The vehicle approached her and she heard a cry of, "Tiny, Tiny." from inside. The dog became alert in an instant. As Caleb halted the 4x4 beside her, Tiny stood on his hind legs, lifted his front paws onto the door and stuck his head in the open window. He tried to lick his owners, by shuffling his back paws and lurching through the window. Caleb got covered in slobber and misplaced licks before Carrie could pull him away. "Well there's no doubt he's missed you," he spluttered, trying to spit out dog slobber and still look composed. The 4x4 carried on up to the barn, as Carrie tried to hold on to a very excited Tiny. By the time she was halfway to the barn herself, Tiny had nearly pulled her arm off, trying to get to his owners.

The gentleman, who introduced himself as Peter, came to rescue her and she thankfully handed him Tiny's lead. They walked together to the barn. Tiny had calmed and was happily walking to heal by then, daft dog. The lady, introduced as Paula, had been made comfortable in a chair, with a bale of straw to elevate her foot and a bag of frozen peas on her ankle. Tiny pulled Peter over to see her and had a pat. He then settled himself by her chair and went to sleep. Caleb finished making them a drink and Jane returned from the field. "What a day," exclaimed Paula, "first hours of walking and worry over Tiny and now I can't walk at all. Thank you so much for looking after him, and for rescuing me from the beach. Are you sure we can't give you a donation for all your help?"

Caleb smiled. "We're really not short of funds, if it's OK, I'll find you some posters to put up in your local area, to let people know we're here. If you'd known about us, you could have made a phone call and saved yourself all that worry. You'll be helping other dog owners if you can help us spread the word."

Peter suddenly stared at Caleb. "It's been bugging me where I'd seen you before, since you rescued us, the penny's just dropped. The voice, that smile, you're Caleb Kirkmichael aren't you? How on earth have you ended up here, on a farm – is this a film set or something?"

"Busted!" Grinned Caleb. "And not a film set, but my new home and animal sanctuary. This has been my dream for years and it's finally coming together.

Carrie's my partner in the farm, and in life. Jane's our vet, Don's our Farrier and Juan, who you haven't met, is our farm manager. So far, we've rescued ten horses and two dogs, so the staff almost outnumber the rescues, but we're thinking big."

"I guess you're not short of a few bob then, thanks for not taking my money."

"Peter!" exclaimed Paula, shocked by her partner's bluntness. The others, including Caleb, just laughed.

"We'll be delighted to distribute some posters for you Caleb, at least Peter will, I might not be very mobile for a day or two. I know it's a bit of a cheek, but can we come back and have a tour round your sanctuary, when I can walk, so we can tell people about it. I belong to lots of clubs and groups that would love to hear about your work."

"Of course you can Paula, we hope to do tours for interested groups soon, when we have some animals to show them. We're working on a website and a Facebook page too, if you use the internet?"

"I do, I'll look out for those, thanks. We'd better get home now Peter, shall I call a taxi?"

Carrie interrupted them, "No need for a taxi, we can take you home. We need to go into town and pick up the posters anyway, if we're going to be able to give you some of them."

Caleb and Peter gently helped Paula back into the 4x4 and got in themselves, Tiny sat happily in the boot. Carrie grabbed her bag, ran a brush through her hair and jumped in the back with Peter. They headed off for town, with Tiny drooling contentedly down Carrie's neck.

Jane and Don sat together discussing the morning's events. The coincidence of meeting Tiny's owners amazed them both. As Jane got up to go back to her work, she bent and kissed Don's cheek. She walked off leaving him touching his cheek in surprise and smiling.

Chapter 18

Harvesting

By the end of June, all the hay was cut, baled and in the barn. Everyone had helped, even Josh came for a weekend of hay carting before he finished at the Scarton practice. The team was shaping up well. Jan started working for the farm in mid-June and Josh was officially starting very soon. A date had been set for Carrie and Caleb's wedding, 14th August, in the village church. Julian had become a staunch supporter of the sanctuary and was spreading the word wherever he went. Two dogs had come for a short stay at the farm, at his request, when an elderly parishioner had been taken into hospital suddenly. The dogs were able to be returned to the parishioner as soon as he was home again and had, no doubt, given him much comfort as he recovered. Julian even found time to walk the pair whilst the chap got stronger at home. The Vicar had also been responsible for their second full dog rescue, when he had a call from a young mother, who's partner had left her. She could no longer afford to feed her dog and her family. She was offered free dog food by Caleb, but she decided she wasn't coping and asked the sanctuary to find the dog, Rufus, a new home. He was a sweet dog, of mixed breeding, with a bit of a boisterous attitude. The first thing they did was castrate him. Without knowing his genetic make-up, it would be irresponsible to let him breed, and they hoped it may quieten him down a little. Jan took charge of retraining him, to make him easier to handle. She had Rufus with her wherever she went and trained him to sit quietly while she worked. Carrie secretly suspected, and hoped, he would end up staying with Jan, they had a strong bond.

They had also taken on three more horses and two nanny goats in June. An elderly man had passed on and left the animals without an owner. All three of the horses were elderly, too old to re-home, so they would live out their days on the farm. They were happily spending the summer in the cliff fields. The goats were young and healthy. Carrie did a bit of phoning to see if any local smallholders might want them, if not they could stay on the farm too. Goats are natural browsers, eating a wide variety of shrubs and hedging, as well as weeds and grass. Juan had used the electric fence to make them a long thin paddock, along a bushy bit of hedgerow, where they could find a variety of plants to eat. They turned out to be quite good at limboing under the bottom strand of the electric fence and escaped a few times. Luckily the whole farm was securely fenced at its boundaries so they couldn't get far. Rounding them up and getting them back in their paddock was another effective team bonding exercise, complete with colourful language! Carrie eventually discovered there was a form of electric netting available that was electrified almost right down to the ground. So far this had been keeping them in more successfully.

Mum and her puppies were still fit and happy. The pups were fully mobile with eyes wide open and looking for mischief. Mum was beginning to get a bit fed up with them clambering all over her and was happy to leave them for longer and longer periods of time. In a team meeting (extended tea break) one day, the puppies' re-homing came up in conversation. Carrie and Caleb had already decided they would like both of the girls, the mostly brown one they were going to call Nutmeg, Meg for short, and the brown and white one was to be Cinnamon, or Cinn. It turns out they were not the only ones wanting to adopt. Jane and Don both wanted a boy each and Juan's wife, who had visited to see the pups, had fallen in love with Mum. Juan planned to take her home as a surprise, having told his wife there was no way they were having a dog. The pups were nearly seven weeks old now so it wouldn't be long before they went their separate ways. Jane would make sure everyone remembered vaccinations and spaying or castrating when the time was right. Mum was already booked to be spayed as soon as the pups were weaned.

Work on the house was coming on faster now, the roof was back in place so the house was watertight Work on the plumbing and electrics was started and coming on slowly. Carrie was still avoiding going inside, but Caleb insisted on giving her an update each day. The planners had given permission for Carrie's outdoor arena, and the groundwork for that had started. It was a large area, forty meters long by twenty wide, which had to be dug out, drainage put in, levelled, sand laid and a membrane laid. Then it was resurfaced with a soft crumbly layer of rubber and sand. This finally gave a durable surface that was never too hard or too soft and never froze or got too wet. In other words, a surface that horses could be ridden on all year round. Big floodlights were fitted on tall poles at each corner to allow riding in the dark. Finally, a tall slatted fence was erected all around the arena to offer a little wind protection and keep horses inside. Carrie and Jane were both really excited to see the arena coming together and couldn't wait to use it.

Carrie's birthday was at the beginning of July. She said she didn't want a party or anything and only asked Caleb for some new yard boots for her present. Her old boots had finally given up, the sole ripping off one, while they were chasing goats. On the day of her birthday she was banned from working and they all ate cream cakes at their morning tea break. She got cards from everyone and a letter inside Dave and Gregg's card asking if they could visit the following week. That was a good present, she missed them so much. Caleb had taken her shopping later in the morning, for a pair of boots, at the shop where they bought his, months before. She chose a pair that were ideal for riding and slogging around a wet farm, she was delighted with them. Caleb insisted she buy some bits for Bilbo, and a lovely new pair of jodhpurs for riding in. While she was looking round, he disappeared and came back with a beautiful bridle that he wanted to buy her, for Bilbo. It was one of the best makes and the leather was wonderfully soft. She thought it was beautiful, but she had a perfectly good bridle for Bilbo. She suggested Caleb buy it for Jaffa instead, Jaffa's tack had been pieced together from stuff Sally no longer needed so it was not as nice as Bilbo's. He agreed and disappeared again. When she finished her browsing there was a good little pile of stuff waiting to be rung through the till. She felt very lucky to be getting so much. Caleb reappeared, just in time to pay. Perfect man! He added a couple of things in bags to the pile, not letting her see them until the bill was paid. He had bought the bridle for Jaffa, but he had bought one for Bilbo to match. She kissed him lovingly, it was a beautiful bridle and a girl can never have too much horse stuff!

After their shopping spree, they had a lovely romantic lunch in a small restaurant overlooking the sea. Caleb was very attentive and made her feel totally loved and spoilt. They returned to the farm mid-afternoon and Carrie found Bilbo and Jaffa tacked up and ready to go out for a ride. Caleb was coming out with her. They rode to the beach and galloped along the sand laughing and racing each other. They decided to see if the horses would go further into the water, which they did willingly. They walked back towards the slipway in the sea, with the horses' chest deep in the water and their own legs soaking wet from dangling in the waves. Luckily, it was so warm, they all enjoyed the cooling seawater. They rode back slowly, letting the horses graze for a bit when they reached the top of the cliffs. After sitting on the grazing horses for a while, chatting away, they decided it was time to head home. As they rode up the drive Carrie could see a horsebox lorry sat by the barns. She said, "Who's that, are we expecting anyone, maybe it's another rescue case?" Caleb just smiled and rode on. They dismounted and looked at the lorry. It was brand new and very posh. Carrie read the writing on the side and gasped. It said 'Cliff Top Animal Sanctuary' with a beautiful logo underneath, an outline of a dog's head and a horse's head intertwined in a Celtic style. All the rest of the team appeared out of the barn, smiling at her expression. Jane came and took the horses from them so Carrie could have a closer look.

"Caleb, it's beautiful, when did you order this? Why didn't I know? Wow, our own horsebox. We can rescue anything from anywhere in this."

"You didn't know, my lovely, because I didn't tell you. It's the last birthday surprise. You can use it to take our own horses to different places to ride, or to shows and competitions if you like. It's for you, and for the sanctuary. It's not huge, as I didn't think you'd want to take an HGV test, but it holds three horses. It has a bit you can sleep in too, and a tiny kitchen, and a toilet. It's a bit like a baby Winnie, with room for horses too. Do you want to look inside?"

"Err, YES! But I am still taking in the outside, it's beautiful." Carrie walked around the lorry admiring the paintwork. The main background colour was a lovely dusky lilac or pastel heather colour. The wording and the logo were a rich deep purple with curly Celtic designs and lines all round the body. The Sanctuary words and logo appeared again on the back and the cab bonnet. The whole thing had a slightly rainbow metallic sheen which made it look very classy.

Caleb said, "I hope you like the colour, I know you love purple. I chose the background colour as it reminded me of the dress you wore the first time we met. It took me ages looking through colour charts to find the colour that matched my memory of that night. The rainbow metallic finish was the boy racer coming out in me, I'm afraid. I saw a sample of the lacquer and fell in love. The logo was a design I've had in my head for years, made presentable by a good designer. I've had headed paper and business cards printed with it on already. I couldn't stop myself. Can we look inside now, pretty please?"

Caleb opened the back ramp first. The horse area was so clean and pristine. The floor was covered in black rubber matting and the rest was white. It looked too good to use, but she couldn't wait to use it nevertheless.

Next, he opened the cab. She clambered into the driver's seat and looked around. There seemed to be everything you could ever want here. There were so many gadgets and buttons. It looked like there was a sat nav and a screen where you could watch the horses travelling in the back. There were, apparently, all round cameras for safe reversing. The seats were dark purple leather as was the steering wheel. It was amazing. And totally crazy. She was speechless.

Caleb practically dragged her out of the cab, he was so excited for her to see the rest. He opened the door to the living area and lifted her in, ignoring the steps altogether. He jumped up behind her to show her all the gadgets inside. There were two double seats, one either side of a small table. One set of seats had hidden seatbelts so an extra two people could travel in here, as well as three in the cab. The seats converted into a double bed somehow, she didn't try it. There was another double bed above the cab. There was a triple kitchen cabinet with a small sink on one cabinet, and an oven and fridge underneath the others. A hob was on top of the oven. There were various cupboards squeezed into other gaps. The seats in here were also deep purple leather. The walls were a very pale lilac and the floor was dark purple rubber. "This is just a totally crazy, beautiful thing. I love it. It's going to get us noticed, that's for sure." Carrie was laughing as she looked around. "It's a mixture of my love of purple gone mad and your love of gadgets on overdrive, it's brilliant."

Caleb looked a bit sheepish, "I might have got a little bit carried away with all the choices, the guy taking the order did keep asking if I was sure about it all! I love it too, but it is a bit 'unique' I guess."

Carrie giggled, "We'll never lose it in the super-market car park, that's for sure. I'll drive it with pride, it has your heart and soul in the design." She hugged him tightly.

When they came out of the horsebox the others were all sitting in the barn. "There's tea here for you guys," shouted Don. They joined the team, who shared their opinions on the horsebox. Views were mixed about the purple, but on the whole, everyone thought it was impressive. Jan had made Carrie a birthday cake so they all enjoyed a slice, despite Carrie and Caleb being stuffed from their lunch. Well, it would be rude not to.

When they lay in bed that night, with a sudden strong wind howling around Winnie in the barn, Carrie cuddled up to Caleb and thanked him for her amazing birthday. They'd been very tempted to sleep in the new horsebox, but Winnie's big comfortable bed had tempted them more. "Josh should be here at 8am, then our team will be complete, for now," said Caleb. "All we need is more animals to keep everyone busy."

Carrie agreed, "Peter and Paula were so keen when we showed them round the other day, I think they'll be spreading the word, far and wide. It was good to see Paula walking again. Our TV interview looked great too, I wonder when they will put that out?"

"They said sometime this week, but it depends what other news they have, I think. It's going on the half-hour local news slot, at tea time, so lots of people should see it. The radio interview I did is going out tomorrow at 3pm, in their countryside programme apparently."

"I think that's enough work talk," said Carrie grinning. "I want my last birthday present!" She rolled over and pounced on Caleb, kissing him as she straddled his hips with her legs. "On second thoughts, maybe I should just let you rest a while, while I thank you for my other presents." She slid down his body, kissing his chest and belly slowly and sensually. By the time she reached the soft skin at the base of his belly, he was holding her head and moaning with urgency. She looked up at him and smiled wickedly. "Thank you, you beautiful, crazy man. I won't say more now though, I was taught not to speak with my mouth full!"

Chapter 19

Loaning

Dave and Gregg arrived for their visit, just as the team were finishing their lunch the following Thursday. The team greeted them like old friends as they arrived, and then dispersed to return to their various jobs. Carrie sat to catch up with her friends over coffee. Caleb would be back soon, having popped to the village. The lads were sporting matching engagement rings and looked really pleased with themselves. "We've set a date for our wedding, it's going to be on the 20th September, at the rugby club in Elver, we hope you can come Carrie, and Caleb of course."

"That's great news, and we'll be there for sure," said Carrie. "Ours is on the 14th of August, here, so we don't clash, thankfully. I really must sort out invites. I hope you two will be here, if you're not too busy shopping for dresses for your own big day?"

Gregg laughed, "I'm never going to live that comment down am I. We have amazing, matching, manly suits with ruffle cuffed shirts and cummerbunds, Dave looks so gorgeous in his. I can't wait. And yes, we'll be here, will Caleb be inviting any of his hunky film star friends?"

"Hey, you're about to be a married man," said Dave indignantly, but with a smile breaking through his stern look. "No more drooling over Caleb's friends. You're mine now."

Carrie listed who she thought was coming, both Dave and Gregg obviously wanted to know, despite Dave's outburst. The lads weren't disappointed with the list.

After a while, Gregg got a serious look on his face and said, "Carrie, we wanted to come and see you today, to catch up, but also to talk about your house. We adore living there, but we feel it's time we bought somewhere of our own, you know, get on the ladder, all that grown-up stuff. I hope you don't mind, but we had your house valued, to see if we could afford it. I remember you saying you might sell it one day. Sadly, and not unexpectedly, we can't stretch our budget to what it's worth. We'll have to find something within our budget, so we wanted to tell you straight away, you may need new tenants."

Gregg looked worried about giving Carrie the news but she was totally supportive of their plans. "Wow, that's really exciting for you both, are you staying in Elver or moving away somewhere exotic?"

"Are you saying Elver isn't exotic?" joked Dave. "All our friends are there, so we want to stay. It's hard to find anywhere decent we can afford though, prices are getting silly. Even with two decent wages, we'll struggle to get more than a tiny estate house."

How much short of the value of my house is your budget?" asked Carrie. "I'd be really happy if you bought it, it holds lots of memories for me."

"The gap is too big Carrie, even if you offered us a good deal, we'd be short. We really hoped we could buy it, but there's just no way the banks will lend us that much, and no way we could afford the monthly repayments, the interest would be a killer."

"OK, let's wait for Caleb and discuss it more later. Who wants to see some cute puppies?" They headed down to the vet centre to visit Mum and her big and boisterous pups. Caleb found them happily sitting under a pile of puppies when he returned. Mum was taking the opportunity to sleep while the pups were entertained, but she jumped up to greet him as he entered the pen. "Hi guys, how are the wedding plans coming along?" Caleb asked as he sat on the floor and got mobbed by the pups.

"20th September, and Carrie says you'll both be there," smiled Dave.

"We certainly will, can we stay at the house or shall I book us a hotel?" he asked. "I expect you will have family who need accommodation too."

"We assumed you'd want to use Carrie's old room, but if you'd rather go to a hotel, we can give it to my parents, they'll be staying for a few days beforehand."

Carrie said, "We'll book a hotel, then they can stay there and be settled. What sort of do are you having, is it formal or relaxed?"

"Definitely relaxed, just a quick meal after the service then dancing the night away. We're going on honeymoon to Cuba for a fortnight the next day, I'm so excited." Dave squirmed nearly as much as the puppies.

Carrie broached the subject of the house, filling Caleb in on what the lads had told her. "What do you want to do Carrie, I'm sure we can help them buy it, if that's what you want?"

Gregg immediately interrupted, "That's very kind of you Caleb, but we need to be independent, I don't want us to start off feeling like we didn't buy a home with our own hard work, it would seem like cheating somehow."

Carrie had expected this response from Gregg, she said, "I understand what you're saying Gregg and I respect your ideals. What about if you borrowed the money from us, instead of having a mortgage. We could offer the loan at a much lower rate of interest and make the repayments more affordable. The length of the loan could be the same, and the house would be yours from the start, but you wouldn't be paying huge profits to a bank for the duration. Have a think about it. We can draw up a contract, with Caleb's lawyers, then you can get a lawyer to check it works for you. I would dearly love you to have the house, so I can still visit it occasionally and relive the good times. You'd be helping me as much as we'd be helping you really."

Gregg looked like he was going to dismiss the idea out of hand when Dave put his hand on Gregg's arm. "Darling, I know I always let you lead in these sorts of decisions, but this is too good an offer to dismiss out of hand. I'm putting my foot down for once and saying we'll think about it, before we let our pride get in the way of our future. Thank you, Carrie, Caleb, we'll get back to you when we've thought it through, if that's OK?"

"That's wonderful," said Caleb, "have you eaten? Let's go to the local pub for a meal and compare wedding plans. I bet you're more prepared than we are!" They headed out in the 4x4 towards the village. After a good meal and some serious wedding talk, they headed back to the farm, where the lads said their goodbyes and got ready to head back to Elver.

Carrie hugged Gregg and whispered, "Think about our offer Gregg, it's not like we're giving you the money, we just want to see you happy and settled. I love that house, thinking of you, still there, would make me feel so content. I can picture you both there and remember how you supported me through my darkest moments."

She then hugged Dave and whispered, "Work on him Dave, I know that house is meant for you."

Caleb hugged both lads too and said, "Please consider our offer. Why should the bank have so much of your hard-earned money, you need it more than them. We'll see you here on the 14th if not before. Come as early as you like, the ceremony's at 2pm, in the church, but lots of people are coming here before lunch. We've booked caterers to keep everyone fed and the bar will be well stocked. If you want to stay, bring a blow-up mattress and some bedding. We have loads of empty rooms in the new buildings, they're nice and warm. The house won't be finished or I'd offer you a proper bedroom."

The lads drove away, waving as they went. Carrie looked sad. "I don't think Gregg will let us help them, I'll probably have to sell the house, or find some new tenants."

"Don't underestimate Dave, I have a feeling he'll talk Gregg around. I hope so. Let's get the lawyers to draw up a draft contract and send it to them, so they can get advice before they decide. That way they can compare costs and see how much they'll save over the years."

Carrie kissed him and thanked him for looking after her friends.

The next day they made themselves sit down and get the last few invites for the wedding sent out. Caleb had contacted his closest film industry friends, and his parents, by email already, as they were spread all over the world. Most were coming. He'd only invited those he really wanted to see, the list would have been endless otherwise. The list included Stephen and Ellie of course. There were about forty others in total, some famous names and some film crew or other film staff, and their partners. He'd asked his PA, Lynne, if she'd like to come, she was keen, so he told her to book her flight on his business account. She was making a holiday of it and planned to spend a few days at the farm, before touring around Britain. He decided he could live with his conscience if he offended any other film people by not inviting them. His parents were coming, of course, and a couple of other family members. He had few friends outside of the industry, his old life had been so wrapped up in the Hollywood set.

Carrie had no family to invite. Her parents and grandparents were all gone and she had no siblings. There was one uncle somewhere, her father's brother, but she'd never met him. He and her father fell out before she was born. Her friends consisted of Dave and Gregg and Sally and Terry. They'd invited all the sanctuary team and the lady from the village shop. Andrew, the estate agent who found Caleb the farm, was coming, with his wife and his Father. Of course Julian the vicar would be there, and Babs was coming from the Mindon sanctuary. Lastly, they decided to invite Paula and Peter as a thank you for the publicity work they were doing.

Caleb had made Carrie leave the booking of caterers and marquees and things to him. He had a contact in the film world who catered for big film sets and could source everything they needed. They had told everyone that the day was to be totally casual, with no suits or designer dresses. They had advised everyone to wear jeans and tee shirts, with a warm jumper and a waterproof coat just in case. They also advised sensible footwear, no high heels and advised boots were packed just in case of rain. Caleb was not convinced all his friends would listen to their advice, but that was their problem. They did buy a small stash of waterproof ponchos and some cheap wellingtons in various sizes for those who came totally unprotected.

The machinery barn would be emptied of everything, including Winnie, to be used as an undercover dining area for the sit-down meal. The other barn was fenced off and out of bounds to protect the hay from discarded cigarettes. The vet centre would be safely locked up but the quarantine centre was being used as makeshift bedrooms. It had one shower and two toilets so there may be queues, but it was only one night. As the building hadn't had any animals in yet, it made an ideal dormitory, it was warm and clean.

Carrie and Caleb had decided they wanted to stay extremely casual with their dress too. Carrie had no wish to have a white dress for a second time. For the actual ceremony they had bought purple tee shirts and hoodies with Bride and Groom written on the back and they both had new tight-fitting faded looking jeans and rugged looking ankle-length black boots. The vicar had agreed to wear jeans too, as long as he could wear his dog collar and a black vicar-ish top. They were not having bridesmaids or best men, or any of the usual traditions. Before the meal, Caleb would make a very short speech and that was it.

Any guests who arrived at the farm early were being ferried to and from the church by coach. Those arriving later would meet them there. The caterers were providing a main, sit-down, meal after the ceremony and would offer chips and fast food type snacks from a catering trailer for anyone wanting to eat at other times, they also had a breakfast selection for people choosing to stay overnight. The tables and chairs for the meal were provided by the caterers too. Even the sit-down meal was casual, with steaks, chops and chicken being cooked on big grills. Salads, roast vegetables and jacket potatoes or chips would be freely available for people to choose from. The bar was provided by the local pub and would be free all day and evening. Caleb had paid them an agreed amount in advance so that they could afford to order huge supplies and be fully stocked and ready for a long day.

There was to be no honeymoon as they were both keen to stay on the farm right now. Winnie would be moved right up to the area near the cliffs, where they had got engaged. They had decided to have their wedding night there, followed by a day of isolation on the cliffs together. The team had been told to manage without them for that day, but that they could be called in an emergency. After that, it would be straight back to normal life. Not having to pack and plan for a honeymoon was a relief to Carrie. Although she enjoyed travelling, the thought of having to rush away straight after the wedding had not appealed to her. The fact that Caleb was in total agreement made it an easy decision. There would be time for a honeymoon when everything here was up and running.

Chapter 20

Neglecting

Everything was planned, as far as possible, for the big day and they had just under a month to go. Josh had started work with them, and was busy with Jan and Jane, familiarising themselves with the new equipment. Josh had proved he was keen, within a few hours, by taking over the Facebook page that Lynne had started, and increasing its audience with local links to pet and equine groups. He was waiting impatiently to take over the running of the website Lynne had set up too. He'd already sent her photos of the new horsebox to add to it. His best idea yet, discussed over a tea break, was for the sanctuary to offer a free dog and cat spaying/neutering promotion on the Facebook page. His idea was to offer people who couldn't, or wouldn't, afford to get their pets neutered, a chance to do so for nothing. Caleb loved the idea and was quite happy for Jane and Josh to plan and implement it. While they were quiet, it was a good time to take on the extra work. An advert was drafted for the Facebook page and shared to all the local pet groups they could find. They also got a short slot on the radio to talk about it, Caleb offered to do the recording, his name would help to grab people's attention.

Within a week they had ten cats and five dogs booked in to take advantage of the offer. Jane and Josh worked through them over three days, with Jan's help wherever needed. Jan was spending most of her time setting up procedures and methods for keeping the place organised and all paperwork manageable. Carrie and Caleb were kept abreast of what she was putting in place, and they quickly realised she was worth her weight in gold. They would have managed somehow to muddle through, but Jan turned administration into an art form. Everything was so well planned and organised and nothing was left to chance or the risk of human error. She made it so simple for everyone to do the right record-keeping at the right time. Now they understood why Jane had wanted her so badly, she made everyone else's job easier.

The people whose pets were neutered over those three days all seemed very impressed with the vet centre. Some of them asked if their animals could come there for other treatments. Jane explained that they were not a normal vet's practice but told them, if they ever couldn't afford to keep their pets healthy, to contact them. The promotion was deemed a great success, hopefully preventing many unwanted litters and potential health problems. They decided it was something they should offer again in a few months.

Within a week of the TV interview airing, they had a call from the local police. They had responded to a report of domestic violence and found a home in a pitiful state, with three dogs in small cages in the garage. The disturbance had been sorted, a man arrested and the woman was taken to hospital. This left the dogs with no one to care for them. The police wanted the dogs removed and assessed, with cruelty charges a possibility, but most of all, they wanted to see the dogs safe for the short term. While the police looked into the legal position with the dogs, the sanctuary fetched them and started to assess their health. Two of them were very underweight, with sores on their skinny, bony bodies from lying in their own mess. The third had a bit more weight on it, but, as well as poor skin, it had a very infected eye, that was closed and weeping pus. They all had flea infestations and sore scabby bald patches where they had been scratching. The police had taken pictures on scene, of their physical condition and their living conditions, but Jane decided she wanted a full photographic record of their poor health and, hopefully, of their recovery. She wasn't totally sure they would all recover.

Josh, Jane and Jan all had a hand in treating the poor dogs. They were bathed and treated for their flea infestations and sores first. Two of the dogs were short-haired but the least skinny one had long dirty matted hair that they had to clip off before they could treat its skin and eye. The poor thing was petrified so they decided to anaesthetise it to do the clipping, and then treat the eye while it was still unconscious. On careful examination of the eye, under anaesthetic, Jane found that the eyeball was so damaged that she needed to remove it. The poor dog must have been in agony, both from the initial injury and from the infection. Once the eye was removed and the eyelids stitched together, they were able to finish treating it's sore skin before it came round. The other two dogs took their treatment well, almost enjoying the bath and skin treatments. They all had worm treatments and other injections that Jane hoped would boost their undermined immune systems. Once they were all finished, and the one-eyed dog was awake, they were assigned pens and left to settle in. A while later they were offered a little food, which they devoured in seconds. A routine of small regular feeds was planned by Jan and a rota set up to administer it. Jane did 3 feeds a day so she could examine them and photograph their recovery. Josh did the other daytime feeds and Caleb or Carrie did a late night one and an early morning one. Josh started taking the three for short walks in between his other jobs.

Mum and her puppies were weaned and going to their new homes. Mum went home with Juan the night the three rescue dogs arrived. Don took his pup home that night too. Jane and Carrie left theirs in the pen together until the next day and then separated them all for a short while each day until they were confident together and confident apart. They decided they could stay in the vet centre until after the wedding when all the excitement had finished and things were back to normal. Don brought his pup back to the centre during the day for the company of the others and took him home at night. Juan's wife was thrilled with Mum and decided to call her Millie, she had finished being Mum now.

Over the next few weeks, the dogs that had been so thin began to look better. Their skin was healing and showing a downy growth of hair on the bald patches. The one-eyed dog was coping very well and didn't seem to have any trouble seeing everything. He just moved his head around a bit more than usual, to see things on his blind side. Josh was like a mother hen with all three, walking them and cleaning up after them religiously. They were really responding to his care and getting more outgoing and confident. Jan had given in to the inevitable and started taking Rufus home every night. He still sat and watched her work every day and enjoyed a run around the farm at lunchtime.

The old horses in the cliff fields were looking well and seemed to be enjoying their peaceful life. Cloud had joined them now and was thriving too. Even the goats had settled in their moveable run. Juan had built them a little hut, to move around with them, as they browsed the hedgerows. Goats hate the rain and they could be seen running for their hut whenever there was a downpour. Monkey was still enjoying his private yard by day and Bilbo and Jaffa called for him as he returned to the field every night.

Carrie hoped this sense of everything being under control would last a few more days, until after the wedding. The long-term weather forecast was promising, lots of dry sunny days and warm evenings. It all just felt a bit too good to be true. She was beginning to panic because there was nothing to panic about! Hopefully, it was just bridal nerves. They had three days left before the big day.

Chapter 21

Escaping

When Caleb's phone suddenly started ringing at 4.30 am on Wednesday morning Carrie knew her sense of panic had been justified. The phone was sitting on the bedside cabinet on Caleb's side of the bed, and she recognised the ring tone straight away. Caleb had thought it was funny to use the theme from 'All Creatures Great and Small'. She reached over Caleb, who was still asleep, and answered the call.

"Hi Carrie, it's Babs from Mindon. I'm really sorry to ring you so early but we've got a bit of a situation here. Our sanctuary has a case of strangles, in a recently arrived horse, and is on lock-down. I'm afraid I won't be coming to the wedding, just in case I carry the infection to your horses, but that's not why I'm ringing. We've just had a call from the police, to say there are two loose horses on the A196, fairly near you, but we can't go and get them because of the strangles. Do you have the means to go and fetch them?"

"Yes, of course, we have a new horsebox so we can be on our way now. Give me directions, or a number for the police, and we're on it. I'll ring you later and tell you how we get on, and you can tell me about the strangles case."

I'll text you the policeman's number, he's got the horses cornered in someone's front garden, all he can do to keep them there is stand in the gateway waving his arms, poor chap. There's no one else he can ring this time of the morning so he rang me. I'll ring him back with your number too, how long do you think you'll be, I think it's about twenty miles from you. Take some headcollars with you by the way."

"Tell him we'll be as quick as we can, but it's going to be half an hour at least. We're setting off as soon as I can wake sleeping beauty here and find the head collars and a bucket of food to tempt the horses. Text the number as soon as you can so we know we are heading the right way. Bye for now."

"Bye and good luck, ring me later."

Carrie was shaking Caleb while she tried to get her trousers on. He woke, annoyingly slowly, mumbling and groaning. "Caleb, get up, we have to go and rescue some horses." She shouted at him. He finally surfaced and groggily asked, "what horses?"

"There's no time to explain, go stick your head under the cold tap, wake up, get dressed and get the horsebox started, I'll explain on the way. I'm driving, at least until you wake up more."

She dashed over to the stables and grabbed a selection of head collars and a couple of ropes. Just as she was leaving the yard she stopped, swore, and went back for a bucket of food and two long lunge ropes. Maybe she wasn't awake either!

Caleb was sitting in the horsebox, wide awake and full of curiosity, by the time she returned. He gave her a smile and a kiss and said, "Where to madam?" as he started the engine. He was definitely more awake than her now, she'd let him do the driving. "Just head towards town, we're headed somewhere on the A196." She looked at his phone, which she'd slipped in her pocket. There was a message from Babs, she dialled the number Babs sent and spoke to the police officer. She assured him they were coming

291

as quickly as they could and asked exactly where they were. The PC asked if she had a sat nav. Apparently, the owner of the garden was out of bed, helping to keep the horses contained, whilst complaining about damage to his herbaceous borders. He gave the postcode to the PC, who passed it on to Carrie. She turned on the sat nav and entered the postcode he gave her. In a minute or two she had an estimated arrival time and a map for Caleb to follow. She told the PC they would be about ten minutes and hung up.

Caleb happily followed the sat nav to the right area and suddenly spied a policeman waving in the dawn light. They pulled up across the driveway, blocking the gateway. Two big grey horses were visible in the garden, happily grazing on the once immaculate lawn. Carrie jumped down with two big head collars and went to catch them. She had a pocket full of horse food to tempt them but they were happy to give in and be caught. She slowly led them towards the horsebox.

While she held the two horses, she asked Caleb to reverse the horsebox into the gateway and drop the ramp at the back. She asked the PC and the owner of the garden to stand and block the gaps between the horsebox and the gateposts just in case one of the horses tried to escape. Horses don't always cooperate when asked to walk into a horsebox, and she had no idea if these two had been in one before. Caleb jumped out of the cab and lowered the ramp. He held one of the horses while Carrie walked the other confidently towards the box. After a second's hesitation, the horse walked calmly up the ramp. Carrie quickly tied him at the front of the box and shut the internal partition to keep him in place. She patted him and gave him a handful of food as a reward for his good behaviour. She came down the ramp and took the other horse from Caleb. Again, she walked confidently up the ramp, hoping this horse would cooperate as well. The rope tightened but the horse fidgeted at the bottom of the ramp, unwilling to go up. Carrie came back down to his head and started again. He dug his heels in a second time and would not go up. Just as Carrie was about to turn him away and try a third time, the horse already in the box neighed loudly. The horse beside her neighed back at him, shot forward and charged up the ramp. He must have decided he wasn't getting left behind. She closed the partition quickly before he could change his mind and charge out again. She tied him up, came back down the ramp and helped Caleb lift and secure it. Caleb turned to the PC and gave him a handful of business cards. "If you find the owners, you can contact us on this number. We'll post that we have them on local equestrian websites too. If they contact us, do you need to know, or is it no longer a police matter? Keep the rest of the cards in case you ever need us again, by the way."

"This gentleman might like to talk to them, regarding the damage to his garden, but it's no longer a police issue really."

Caleb turned to the property owner. "OK, if you give me your number, sir, I'll pass it on to the owners, in the hope they do the right thing and contact you. We can't do more than that though." Both men thanked them for coming so quickly and wished them luck with the horses. Each man was staring at Caleb with a dawning sense of recognition. Caleb waved and drove away quickly before either man had a chance to ask any questions, 5.30 in the morning was too early for autographs and long chats.

As they drove home, Carrie turned on the screen connected to the camera in the horse area. A picture of two calm and happy horses swaying with the movement of the horsebox appeared. "I love this horsebox," said Carrie happily. As they reached the farm they discussed where to put their new additions. Hopefully, they wouldn't be here long. Carrie was keen to keep them quite separate from the rest of the horses. Although there was no reason to believe they were infected, strangles was a very contagious disease and, if it was in the area, she didn't want to take any risks. She thought of the quarantine field but decided to keep that clean for now. They chose a field at the far side of the farm, acres away from the rest of the horses. Caleb had a quick walk around the field to check the fences and the water trough. Carrie opened the back ramp ready to unload the horses. She spoke to them as she opened up, to calm them, but they seemed quite happy, enjoying the adventure. By the time Caleb returned she was leading the first horse down the ramp. Caleb held the first horse close to the box, while she unloaded the second one. She didn't want either of them panicking, thinking they were being left alone. Once both horses were standing in the field, and the gate was shut, they let them go. The horses galloped off, bucking and snorting, to investigate their new home.

Carrie and Caleb returned to the barn for a cup of tea and a relax, the early call had them both a bit frazzled. At least it had gone smoothly, thank goodness the grey horses were so well behaved. They wondered about returning to bed, but it was 7am already, so there wasn't much point. They both had a shower and a change of clothes and got ready for the day.

Within half an hour the rest of the team started to arrive. Caleb and Juan set themselves the task of getting an old pressure washer working, so they could clean and disinfect the horsebox. Carrie wasn't sure if it was the chance to play with water or the pride in the new box that was their motivation, but they both set off with enthusiasm. She was glad the box would be clean and safe to use again, so she didn't ask questions. Josh agreed to spread the word about the two grey horses on social media, as soon as he'd seen to the dogs in the vet centre. Jan and Jane headed out to check all the other horses and the goats. Carrie found herself alone with her thoughts. Don was out shoeing some horses for one of his old clients, she decided to text him and get him to spread the word about the greys too. Someone might recognise the description. She sent off the text, then sat and thought about their fast-approaching wedding day. She couldn't believe how lucky she was, becoming Mrs Kirkmichael in a couple of days.

This time last year, she was still telling herself she didn't deserve to feel love. Now, here she was, with a man who rocked her world and a new life, it was like nothing she could have imagined in her wildest dreams. She felt so blessed. She sent a silent message of love to her dead husband Matt. She knew he would approve of her new life. She thought of Don and his grief at losing his wife. He seemed so much better these days, and definitely in love with Jane, even if he couldn't admit it to himself yet. She hoped he would push himself to jump that last hurdle, Jane deserved to feel his love.

Chapter 22

Falling

Josh sat himself at a computer waiting for it to boot up. He'd walked the dogs to the grey horse's field and taken a photo of them on his phone. It was a bit of a distant shot as he'd stayed outside the field. All the talk of strangles that morning had him worried. He uploaded the photo and went onto their Facebook page. He typed out a post about the horses, stating where they were found, and added the photo. He shared it to every local group and page he could find, in the hope the owners, or someone else who knew the horses, would see it. He added the sanctuary's emergency phone number, Jan had the phone, he'd checked.

Carrie shook herself out of her thoughts and decided she would get Monkey settled in his yard, then see if anyone needed her help. She was just filling up a bucket of water for Monkey, who was happily standing on the hose and trying to look innocent, when her phone rang. She answered it as she walked back to the barn. "Hi Don, did you spread the word about our new arrivals?"

"Hi Carrie. Yes, and someone thinks they know who they belong to, she's ringing them now. Shall I pass on your number or the emergency one?"

"Either's fine, and that's great news. Hopefully, they can pick them up straight away."

"Hang on Carrie, she's off the phone, I'll get news." Don went quiet for a couple of seconds then came back. "She can't get an answer on their phone so she's texting them – maybe they're out searching or something. While you're on the phone can I ask a favour? Can we have another chat later today, when I get back to the farm? I need my agony aunt again."

"Of course Don, anytime, you know that. We'll find a private place somewhere, just shout me when you're back."

"Thanks Carrie, and I'll let you know if we get an answer to the text before I leave. Bye for now."

Carrie pocketed her phone and wondered what

was worrying Don, they hadn't had a private chat for weeks. She headed off to find Caleb and Juan, hoping she could be useful helping them. She needed to be busy, but with all these members of staff working so well, she felt a bit surplus to requirements. Everyone was becoming so efficient. Caleb was loving learning from Juan and went off every morning like an excited child. When she arrived here, she had a purpose, but now she was beginning to feel a bit lost and rudderless. She shook herself, what was she thinking? She had the best life, and here she was looking at the negative side, she must find her own purpose and stop feeling sorry for herself. She hoped it was just bridal nerves clouding her emotions.

Just as she was walking down to the vet centre to find Caleb, a car pulled up at the gate. A woman got out of what was obviously a taxi, leant in to pay the driver, dragged out a holdall and headed through the gate. The woman was stunning. She was tall and slender, with amazing blond hair flowing around a gorgeous painted face. She wore a long-fitted coat that cinched in at her ridiculously thin waist. On her feet, she wore super high heels that flattered her long stockinged legs. Carrie was just thinking she must be one of Caleb's film star friends, here early for the wedding, when she saw Caleb running out of the vet centre. He ran towards the woman, arms outstretched, hugged her, picked her up and swung her around before gently putting her down and kissing her. Carrie watched, her mouth agape, as the two of them walked, arm in arm, back into the vet centre. She had never seen Caleb greet anyone, except herself, with such feeling. She suddenly felt cold, and even less like she had a role to play here. Who was that woman, and why did she, Carrie, the bride, not know why her future husband had greeted her so lovingly? She turned around and headed back towards the courtyard. Suddenly she needed to be as invisible as she was feeling today. She grabbed Bilbo's tack, a riding hat and a brush and walked towards his field. She'd go for a ride and sort her head out, before she had to meet superwoman, whoever she was. Within a very few minutes, she was on Bilbo's back and heading up the track to the cliffs. She knew she could get on to the road, by following the track along the cliff. She didn't want to meet anyone right now. She rode past the spot where they got engaged. For some reason that brought tears to her eyes, she shook them away. "I really need to have a stern word with myself!" she said to Bilbo. "What is wrong with me today? All I can do is doubt my own worth and doubt if anyone needs me, even Caleb. I need to get over this, I feel like I'm grieving again, I haven't felt this unsure of myself for months." Bilbo didn't seem to have any words of wisdom for her, but just being on his back felt like a tonic. They met up with the road and headed to the beach. When they reached the sand Bilbo started jogging, anticipating a good gallop. Carrie let him have his head and enjoyed the speed as he thundered along the tide line. This was a great way to clear her emotions. They galloped for what felt like miles before Bilbo started to slow. She started to pull him up, when he suddenly stumbled and pitched her over his head, as he tried to keep his balance. She landed on the wet sand, on her shoulder and head, and just lay there, stunned and shocked. For a good few moments she couldn't think at all. Her head spun and her shoulder ached. Bilbo had stopped a little way further on and was looking back at her, no doubt wondering why she was lying on the ground. He wandered nearer and came to a stop, looking down at her. She reached out with her good arm and grabbed his reins. He seemed OK, but she couldn't really concentrate on anything. She just lay there trying to think about what she should do.

After what seemed like forever, or no time at all, she started to think a bit more clearly. She needed to get home. She needed to check Bilbo was OK. She needed to sit up. Which one first? Maybe she could just lie here a bit longer?

She waited a few more minutes and things started to clear again. She gently grabbed Bilbo's nearest leg and pulled herself into a sitting position. He stood very still, even when she dropped his reins, almost as if he knew she needed him. Carrie spoke to him as she sat there, trying to keeping his interest, and reassured that she could speak in coherent sentences. Her shoulder didn't feel too bad, she tried moving it around. It ached, but everything moved and nothing went crunch – a good sign. Slowly she tried to stand, still using Bilbo for support. Her head started to spin again and she leant into Bilbo's shoulder until the dizziness stopped. Phone – she had a phone, she should call someone. Did she really need to worry anyone, she'd be all right in a minute. No, she should phone, let them know she was here, so they knew to check she got home. She pulled out her phone and selected Caleb's number. She waited and waited but it didn't ring. She looked at the screen, it was only then her thoughts gathered together and reminded her, there was no signal on the beach.

Bilbo was just beginning to fidget a bit, he was ready to go home now, please. She gathered her thoughts again. She checked his legs, he didn't seem injured. She got brave and took a couple of steps. Her head spun a bit but she was OK. Bilbo walked beside her and didn't limp, he was OK. She decided trying to get back on him was beyond her for now, but she could walk home. They wandered along the beach together, Carrie's head clearing more as they went. She tried to look ahead, see the slipway up to the road, but it was still too far away. Never mind, one foot in front of the other, we'll get there. After another ten minutes, she could see the slipway, although it seemed miles away. She felt strong enough to try and mount Bilbo now, so she looked around for something to stand on, to give her a bit more height. With a sore arm, she didn't think she could get on from the ground. She headed up the beach, nearer to the base of the cliffs. Here she found some rocks and tried to climb on one. Next thing she knew she was back sitting on the floor. She got up and tried again. This time she got on the rock, now to get Bilbo near enough to get on his back. She encouraged him nearer, he wasn't sure about the rock, it had a slightly evil look and he'd rather not get any closer, thank you very much. She pulled his reins a bit and talked to him. "Bilbo, I need your help here, stop being a drama queen and come closer!" After a few moments eyeing up the rock, Bilbo finally stepped nearer. Carrie took her opportunity, grabbed the stirrup, stuffed her foot in and hauled herself up into the saddle. By the time she was sitting up, the world was spinning again, but she was on board. She asked Bilbo to walk on and headed for the slipway. At one point she tried a trot, but her head spun so much she nearly came off again. Walking would have to do.

Eventually, the slipway seemed close. Bilbo was trying to trot again, impatient to get home. She held him back but she was struggling, with one arm feeling weak and sore. She was just beginning to wonder if she should get off and walk again, feeling dizzy and faint, when she heard an engine and looked up the slipway. Thank goodness! The farm's 4x4 was driving down towards her. She stopped Bilbo and decided to dismount. As she leant forward and swung her leg over the back of the saddle everything went black. She came round lying on the floor with something soft under her head. It was Don! "Hi Carrie, how are you feeling? What hurts?"

"Hi Don. What are you doing here? Why am I on the floor? Where's Bilbo?"

"Bilbo's fine, he's grazing halfway up the slipway.

You fell over when you got off him and seemed to be unconscious, but you didn't hit your head, I was watching, you just passed out or something. Can you remember?"

"I fell off earlier. I think I landed on my head then. I've been trying to get home but I was too dizzy to go fast. Maybe that's why I fell over? I saw you coming and tried to get off to talk to you. I think I need a sleep, can you take me home?"

"Oh Carrie, I think we need to get you to hospital. Can you stay here on your own while I go up to the top of the cliff and ring someone? I can't get a signal here, I tried before you woke up."

"OK, I'll just close my eyes for a minute. Don't let Bilbo run away. I need to ride him home." Carrie seemed to pass out again before Don could do anything. He gently stood up, supporting Carrie's head and trying to keep it still. He took off his shirt and gently laid her head on it. Bilbo was now standing behind the 4x4, he would have to move him, to be able to move the vehicle. Instead, he jumped up into Bilbo's saddle and galloped him up the slipway to the top. As soon as his phone picked up a signal he dialled 999 and asked for an ambulance. Next, he dialled Jane and told her to bring Caleb down to the slipway urgently. They had been searching for Carrie, around the farm, for an hour, before they realised Bilbo was gone and that she might be on the beach. Caleb had been beside himself with worry, they all were, but Caleb was a mess.

As soon as he'd talked to Jane, he turned Bilbo around and returned to Carrie as fast as he dared, down the steep slope. She was awake again when he got there and smiled as he leaned over her. "Hi Don, where am I, my head hurts, can you help me get up?"

"Hi Carrie, you should stay there and keep still my love, you've hurt your head. Caleb is coming, and the ambulance."

"Caleb has another woman now, he won't want me. That's why I need to go home. Will you look after him for me?"

"Carrie, I think you're hallucinating. Caleb was frantic, not knowing where you'd gone, he doesn't have another woman. He loves you. Stay awake lovely, help is coming."

Carrie seemed to pass out again and was still unconscious when Caleb and Jane arrived, followed a few minutes later by the ambulance. Caleb was lying beside Carrie, holding her hand and talking to her, as the paramedics reached them. Tears were streaming down his face as he begged her to wake up. Jane had told him, in no uncertain terms, not to move her, checked her airway and breathing then hugged Don and waited. The paramedics took over Carrie's care immediately and soon had her in a collar, on a trolley and in the ambulance. Don told them what little he knew and Caleb sat in the ambulance ready to go.

After the ambulance left, Don reversed both of the farm vehicles up the slipway as Jane went to catch Bilbo. She checked him over and led him up to the vehicles at the top. Don was sitting in the 4x4, with his head in his hands, as she reached him. She took his hand and held it as he sat. He said, "She looked so pale lying there. I didn't know what to do, I galloped poor Bilbo up the slipway so my phone would work. Will she be OK?"

Jane pulled him to his feet and hugged him tight. "I'm sure she'll be fine, thanks to you, you did all you could for her. She's in good hands, she'll just need to rest I expect." Jane looked up at Don as they held each other. Don looked down into her eyes and relaxed a little. He dipped his head and lightly kissed her on the lips. She returned the kiss, with gentle trepidation. Don kissed her again, deeper this time, soon they were sharing kisses and holding each other like they were really meant to be together. Eventually, Jane pulled away, smiling. "We need to get this poor horse home to his friends, and I need a cup of very strong tea. Please can we do that again though, it's been a long time coming."

Don laughed, "I'm sorry, you've been very patient with me. Sometimes it takes a big shock to make you realise you should quit fannying around and seize the moment. We never know how many chances there'll be in life. I still have a way to go in my healing, but I'm ready to heal with you, if you'll have me Jane?"

"I'll think about it!" she said winking. "Now give me a leg up onto this horse and I'll race you back." She gave him another kiss. Don followed her slowly back to the farm in the 4x4, not taking his eyes off her for a second and smiling to himself.

Chapter 23

Resting

Carrie finally came round again a few hours later. She was lying in a hospital bed, with Caleb sitting beside her holding her hand. "Hello my gorgeous girl," he said when he saw her eyes open, "how are you feeling?" He stood and bent over to kiss her lips.

"Hi lovely, I'm sorry if I worried you, I feel much better now." She was feeling more herself, her mind was pretty clear and she remembered why she was there.

"I was so worried when no one could find you, then, when I saw you lying on the slipway, I thought I was losing you, my heart was breaking." He was crying again, she squeezed his hand and tried not to cry too.

"Have the doctors examined me yet? Have I done any damage? Can we still get married?"

Caleb laughed softly. "Oh my lovely Carrie, nothing will stop me marrying you – even if we have to squeeze the guests in here! You're going to be absolutely fine, they did loads of tests. You have concussion, and will have a stiff shoulder for a while, but nothing's broken and your head will mend. They think you must have hit a rock, you have a big lump near the base of your skull, just below where your riding hat would have been. That's probably why you were a bit gaga for a while, apparently. You can come home in another twelve hours, as long as nothing changes. You're not allowed out of my sight until we're married now. And you're not allowed to do anything except rest for days and days, maybe weeks! My rules."

Carrie grinned. "What about our wedding night? I must rest, apparently."

"Bugger, shot myself in the foot with my own rules! We'll think of something I'm sure."

Carrie smiled. "Oh Caleb, I love you, I had such a feeling of unease this morning, doubting myself, wondering if I was enough to keep you happy. I went for a ride to clear my head and sort myself out. I should have told someone I was going, but I saw that woman arrive and saw you greeting her so lovingly. I suddenly felt like I wasn't good enough, like I didn't have a role here. It's hard to explain but everyone else on the farm has a role, I'm not sure if I'm a necessary part of it anymore. I wondered if I had been kidding myself all these weeks, wondered if I deserve what we have.............."

"Stop Carrie." Caleb was standing and leaning over her again. "Don't EVER doubt your worth. You are my life, I would give up everything I have to keep you. I thought my dream of the farm was what I needed to be happy, and it does make me very happy, but it would mean nothing without you, my love. When you were lying there unconscious, I didn't know how I'd survive. I thought my heart would stop beating if............" He couldn't say any more, so he lay down on the edge of the bed and held her tight.

"Oh, Caleb, I'm so sorry I worried you. And so sorry I got lost in my emotions, I haven't done that for months. I felt like I was grieving again, and I didn't know why. Then I saw you hugging that woman and felt jealous, I suppose. Just when I was coming to find you for a hug, you were hugging someone else, like you hug me, with passion. I had no idea who she was, she was beautiful, classy and you looked so happy to see her. Who was she, and why didn't I know someone so important to you was arriving?"

"I'm so, so sorry, Carrie, I totally forgot to tell you she was arriving today, she's Lynne, my PA. We've always been close, but not in the way you were thinking, you daft mare! We grew up together, in a way. She was the first person who befriended me, aged fourteen, when we arrived in the US. She's three years younger than me, we were neighbours. There weren't many kids where we lived, so we spent quite a lot of time together. When I first needed staff, when I got successful, my mother suggested I offer her a job. I did, and she's been my PA ever since. We're like siblings. I don't know why I never told you this, and I'm really sorry, but it all seemed like part of my past. I didn't realise how much I missed her until I saw her this morning."

"OK"

"Just OK?"

"I'm sad, that you never told me more about someone so important to you. Now I understand, I'm glad she looked after you all those years. I'm also very glad she's 'like a sister' – I'm not sure I could compete with those legs, and that hair, she's a beauty. Did you two never, you know, get together."

"I'm not her type, love. Although I did try once, when I was nineteen."

"How could she refuse such a young stud?"

"Erm, I didn't have boobies and a fufu, she bats for the other team. She's never really 'come out' to the world, but she knows what she wants, and it was never me."

Carrie laughed, "That must have bruised your nineteen-year-old ego, good for her!"

"My nineteen-year-old ego thanks you for your concern! I think I got over it pretty quickly, I was just starting out with my first film, and surrounded by beautiful actresses, I wasn't heartbroken for long!"

"OK, I get the picture, no more jealousy from me. Shouldn't you be back at the farm keeping her company, she's our guest?"

"Like I said, I'm not letting you out of my sight until you're my wife. I'm sitting here until they let you come home. I spoke to Lynne, and the others, while you were being examined. They are managing fine without us. The grey horses are leaving later, their owners rang earlier. Jane is going to grill them when they arrive, check they are definitely the rightful owners. They sounded very relieved that they were safe. I gave them the garden guys number and they said they would offer him some compensation, I hope they do. All the other animals are fine, including Bilbo. Jane rode him home from the beach and says he is none the worse for his adventure. It sounds like Lynne and Jan are talking admin and comparing notes on good systems, they'll be happy. The catering team have arrived to start setting up their stuff, and Juan is rushing around making everything look neat and tidy. He even has Josh strimming around the pond! So all you need to do is rest and relax, with me for company."

"I can do that anywhere, can you smile sweetly at a nurse and get us out of here quicker, I want to go home."

"No, you're here until the doctor says you're fit to go home, I'm not taking any chances. You are stuck

315

here and stuck with me, so get used to it my girl!"
Caleb grinned.

"Oh, I love it when you're so masterful, it makes
me hot with desire. Shame I have to rest really!" She
grinned back, enjoying his discomfort at that
thought.

Carrie slept for a few hours, Caleb sat and
watched her breathing, just glad that he still had her.
He had no words, even in his own mind, to describe
the feeling when he thought he might lose her. He
suddenly felt deep empathy for what Carrie and Don
had been through, losing their partners. He had felt a
few moments of it today and it had felt like he was
shattering into a million pieces. They had both lived
through the reality of actually losing that person.
How did they ever get whole again? He would be
grateful to Don for the rest of his life for finding
Carrie and caring for her. His love and admiration
for Carrie knew no bounds. He didn't think he could
ever be that strong.

Later that evening, there was a knock on the
hospital room door, Don and Jane poked their heads
inside. "Can we visit, or is Carrie too tired?"

Carrie smiled, "Come in, come in, I've been asleep for ages, I'm fine now. How are you both, I'm sorry I scared everyone. Thanks for finding me Don, and keeping me safe. How's Bilbo, Jane, is he really OK? He took quite a stumble, that's why I fell off, he landed on his knees, nearly went over with me. How's Lynne, is she on her own? Caleb, you need to go home, poor girl."

She looked up and wondered why everyone was laughing at her. "What, what did I say?"

Caleb tried to hug her, but he was laughing so hard, she moved away in a huff. "I'm not hugging you until you stop laughing at me. What did I do?"

Jane came and kissed Carrie's cheek, on the other side of the bed from Caleb. "Thank God you're back to normal. I never felt so glad to hear one of your crazy, rambling monologues. I counted 16 different points and questions in that one! I'll respond in the order you said them. Thanks, we will come in, we're glad you had a good sleep, and that you are fine now, we are both fine, thanks, apology accepted, don't do it again please, Don says you're welcome, Bilbo's fine, he's really fine, I wondered what unseated you, Lynne is fine, playing with dogs, Josh volunteered to stay tonight and keep her company, good luck with getting Caleb to leave your side. I think that was everything!"

Carrie smiled, then giggled, then laughed, until her head and shoulder hurt. It didn't take long. "OWOWOW, don't make me laugh, did I really say all that? Do I do that a lot then?"

Caleb caught her in a hug, while she was distracted. "Stop, breathe my love, don't hurt yourself. And, yes, you do have a habit of trying to get all your words out at once. I love it, it means you are happy, enthusiastic and full of life. Sorry we laughed, I think we're all relieved to see you back to your normal self again."

Don said, "Last time I heard you speak, you thought Caleb had another woman so you were going home, on Bilbo, because he didn't need you, and I was to look after him for you. You were making no sense at all. At least this monologue was based in reality. It's so good to hear your normal crazy, instead of the insane crazy, if you see what I mean."

"Aww, you say the nicest things, Don," Carrie said, with some sarcasm, although she was smiling as well.

Jane added, "It's just good to see you conscious. We were all worried."

They chatted for a few more minutes and then Jane and Don headed off. Carrie looked tired again so Caleb lay down beside her, took her in his arms and suggested they both sleep. When he woke later, it was to see three nurses and a young doctor peeping around the door and quietly arguing as to whether it really was Caleb Kirkmichael sleeping in their ward. He quickly shut his eyes and pretended to still be asleep. Much later, he woke again, to find Carrie stirring in his arms. "Hello sweetie," he said, "did you sleep well?"

"I think so, I don't remember much after we settled down. What time is it, can we go home yet?"

Caleb looked at his watch. "I think it's nearly time, shall I go and see if I can find a doctor and ask?" She nodded. He got up carefully, mindful of Carrie's sharp intake of breath as he moved her. He went to the sink and splashed some water on his face, then headed out to the ward desk.

When he returned to the room, twenty minutes later, he had a doctor and a nurse in tow. They were all chatting like old friends. Carrie sat up, wincing, and smiled at them, trying to look perfectly fit and well. "Can we go home now?" she asked.

The doctor looked at her and smiled. "Let's do a few checks and get your prescription, then, all being well, you can go. Your husband has kindly signed about forty autographs for the children in the ward opposite, and a few for the staff, so I think he has earned you a free pass."

"He's not my husband, until Saturday, you see, I have to get home and get everything ready for our wedding day." The doctor looked at Caleb for confirmation, wondering if this was another semi-conscious ramble from Carrie.

"Don't worry," laughed Caleb, "she's quite sane! We are getting married in two-days time. This was pretty bad timing really, thank goodness all she needs is rest. I won't let her do a thing until Saturday, I'm not risking a relapse. I'll tie her to a chair if necessary."

"We'll pretend we didn't hear that," laughed the

doctor. "I think I'm supposed to report threats of domestic abuse!" The nurse took Carrie's blood pressure as the doctor looked in her eyes and examined her bump. They asked her a few questions, checked she knew the date and where she was, then left to get some medication for her. Caleb sat and put his arm around her. "How are you really feeling sweetie. I can see when you're putting a brave face on, are you sure you feel ready to leave the hospital?"

"I'm fine my love, I ache, but I'll ache just as well at home. All I need is rest, as you said."

He held her close until the nurse returned with her prescription of pain killers. As soon as he had gone, Carrie was looking for her clothes. They were in a pile on the cupboard by the bed, and they were covered in sand, but she didn't care. "Can you help me dress, Caleb, I'm a bit useless." He gently helped her into her trousers and slid her arms into her tee-shirt. She didn't bother with her bra or socks, just stuffed them in her pockets and slipped her feet into her boots. "Let's go home, please." They made their way, slowly, to the main entrance of the hospital and Caleb called a taxi.

Chapter 24

Wedding

The morning of the wedding couldn't have been better. The sun was shining, the forecast was really good and Carrie managed to get out of bed without Caleb's help. She spent the whole day yesterday reclining on a sun lounger in the barn, watching everybody else rush around to get the farm ready for the wedding. Every time she got up to help, someone ratted her out to Caleb, and he came and made her lie down again. She had drunk way too much tea, as everyone made her a cup whenever they stopped for one. All the team seemed to be taking turns to come and sit with her, she was hardly alone for more than ten minutes at a time. Lynne was lovely, checking up on her every little while, and bringing their puppies out to see her every few hours. She turned out to be a very down to earth and friendly person. Not the sophisticated socialite Carrie had expected. Lynne had Carrie in stitches describing Josh's attempts to chat her up the previous night. She had let him down gently, admitting to him, that, whilst he was lovely, she was more likely to get amorous with Jane or Jan. Apparently, he took it well, and they spent the rest of the evening playing computer games, which she won hands down.

By mid-morning of the wedding day, everything was in place and Carrie and Caleb were enjoying sitting together in the sun. Winnie was up on the cliffs, and the barn seemed empty without her, despite being full of tables, chairs and catering equipment. Some of Caleb's friends had arrived early, having flown into Heathrow overnight. They had staked claim to a couple of rooms in the quarantine building and were sleeping off their jet lag, on inflatable mattresses. Caleb had been out to buy loads of mattresses, in a panic, at the last minute. He also bought the shop's total supply of sleeping bags and umpteen pillows. If that was the only thing they had forgotten, it would be a miracle.

The caterers were the only ones working hard now, everyone else was either at home getting ready, travelling, or here enjoying the sun and waiting for the ceremony. Everybody here, so far, was in casual clothes, mostly jeans and tee shirts. Lynne was in leggings and a huge baggy sleeveless shirt, which managed to make casual look anything but.

Carrie had walked round to see the horses first thing, they all looked happy and blissfully unaware of the big day. Monkey was getting a rare day out in the field, to keep him away from gullible victims, who might feed him the wrong sort of stuff. He was a great actor, he could convince anyone he was starving. They were not stopping people from wandering around the farm today, just locking any buildings that were not needed and keeping the animals away from the excitement. By 1pm the field was buzzing with people, some eating, many drinking and all sounding happy and relaxed.

Caleb and Carrie had made their way back to Winnie, on the cliffs, to get changed and freshen up. Carrie's phone rang just as they were about to shower, it was Babs.

"Hi Carrie, don't panic, I'm not sending you on a rescue mission today! I just wanted to wish you both well, and say we will be at the church after all. I felt so sad to be missing out, because of the strangles. So, we'll be there, but we won't come near you, we'll sit at the back and head home once you are wed."

"Oh Babs, that's wonderful. We won't get a chance to talk, but at least we'll know you're there. Thank you. Caleb will phone you once we are back to work, bye for now."

Carrie explained to Caleb and he smiled. "We must give them a wave, if nothing else, I'm so glad she'll be there, she's been so much help to us."

Carrie was managing well with her stiff shoulder, and her head was feeling like her own again. She had a little help getting into her new jeans and tee-shirt, but, apart from that, she could do everything herself. Caleb looked fabulous in his tight jeans and skinny tee shirt. All the manual work he was doing had toned him up beautifully, and he had a great natural tan. From the sensuous kiss she got, when she was in her own tight jeans, she guessed Caleb thought she looked OK too.

The guests would be getting in the coach, about now, to head to the church. Caleb said he'd arranged some transport for the two of them, so they sat out-side and waited to be picked up. Caleb checked the rings were in his pocket for the hundredth time and Carrie jiggled in her seat, feeling the nerves. "When's the transport coming? we can't be late," she said, in a stressy voice.

"Don't worry, they won't go ahead without us!" laughed Caleb. Just as Carrie thought she'd explode with nerves, she heard the sound of hooves coming up the track.

"Ooh, are we riding to church? That could be hard in these tight jeans, you might have to winch me into the saddle," she joked.

She looked along the track, expecting to see Bilbo and Jaffa coming. Instead, she saw two beautiful and immaculately plaited Piebald cobs, pulling a wonderful old farm cart, all decorated with wild flowers, wheat sheaves and corn dollies. She knew immediately, the horses were Carl and Bud, looking stunningly well. She turned and hugged Caleb. "Thank you, they look amazing, it's so good to see them looking that well. It's a perfect old cart too, did Pat have it already? I don't imagine most brides would appreciate it, but I do."

"I knew what sort of cart I wanted to buy and Pat found it and did it up for us. We can keep it here, or sell it again afterwards. It fits Bud and Carl perfectly, they look wonderful, don't they? I think I might have to lift you in though, I don't want you to hurt yourself." Carrie had a minute to greet the horses and have a cuddle, then Caleb gently lifted her into the cart. He climbed up beside her and they sat on straw bales in the back. Pat greeted them warmly and asked, "Ready?" She told the horses to walk on, they headed out to the road and trotted on into the village. When they neared the church, they were amazed to see hundreds of people lining the street. It seemed word of the wedding had spread, all the village were there to wish them well, and catch a glimpse of Caleb and his famous friends! As they pulled up, there were cheers from the crowd. Caleb jumped down and lifted Carrie from the cart. They gave Carl and Bud a hug before heading into the churchyard.

The church was full, with people standing at the back. Carrie looked around in wonder, she knew their invited guests would only fill about half the pews. She caught sight of the stewards from the bonfire party, one of them giving her a shy wave. There was Babs, smiling and dabbing her eyes, with her horsebox driver beside her. Carrie waved and blew them a kiss. The other side of the aisle she saw Stephen and Ellie, no surprise there, but next to them were a few faces she knew but couldn't place, suddenly the penny dropped, they were friends from college she hadn't seen for years. As she looked around she saw the old chap, whose dogs they had looked after earlier in the year, and even some of the builders who had worked at the farm. She imagined the rest were villagers who had squeezed in. She felt so blessed, people had taken time to come and see them on their special day. Even if some of them had probably been expecting a big posh wedding, not them in jeans! She was so glad Caleb had invited some film star friends, at least the villagers would enjoy identifying the famous faces.

They walked up the aisle together and greeted Julian, who was waiting to make them husband and wife. The service was mostly traditional, with a few words added to personalise their vows to each other. They both promised to keep each other in their hearts forever. As they said their "I do's" and Julian pronounced them man and wife, Carrie and Caleb kissed like no one was watching, lost in their own joy at finally being together in the ultimate way. In the end, Julian had to cough loudly to bring them back to the here and now.

They headed out of the church, holding hands and laughing. The crowds were still there and gave them another cheer as they appeared at the door. Lynne was taking photos and bossed them around, into a few poses, before they headed back to the cart. As they left the churchyard a storm of confetti hit them, thrown from all sides. Carrie had a small panic about littering the village, then she looked and realised all of it was oats, and other seeds, bird food, perfect. Even Bud and Carl were putting their heads down and trying to get a free feed. Lynne took loads of shots of them in the cart, then they started the journey back to the farm, waving at people as they went. This time the horses took them in the main gate and into the front field, dropping them off at the bar. Caleb lifted his new bride out of the cart and made her sit, in-state, in her reclining chair, to rest and drink alcohol. Who was she to complain? As the coach of guests pulled in through the gates, Carrie and Caleb were sitting, with pints of cider in their hands relaxing in the sun.

Both the meal and the evening were relaxed affairs. Caleb made a short but heartfelt speech about how lucky he felt to be married to such a wonderful woman, and thanked everyone for supporting them. He also told them about Carrie's little accident, and asked them to allow her to sit and rest all evening. He suggested that everyone come and chat to them, as they sat by the bar, rather than he and Carrie circulating. Everyone seemed to understand, and a circle of bales had appeared round Carrie and Caleb's chairs when they returned to the field. Caleb laughed and said it would be like holding court. Some people danced, some chatted. No one had to sit in a certain place, eat with a certain fork, or worry about who had the best dress. It was just a fun evening. Caleb's parents sat at the periphery of the celebration looking a bit bemused, but everyone else just piled in and enjoyed the fun. Carrie and Caleb spent most of the evening sitting exactly where they started, near the bar. Just about everyone came passed and chatted with them at some point.

For a while, Caleb was deep in conversation with someone Carrie assumed was a show biz friend. She was chatting with Dave and Gregg, so she didn't take a lot of notice. Dave had just told her that they would welcome her and Caleb's help, with a loan to buy her old house. She was over the moon. Later, Caleb told her that the man he had been chatting with was a film producer friend of his. Caleb had just been offered his dream role, in a film being made early the next year. He could practically name his price, they wanted him that badly. The script was one he'd seen, and loved, ages ago but the film rights had never been taken up, until now. He was so excited to be singled out for the role, and Carrie was right behind him when he said he wanted to accept it. When Martyn and Julie Silverdale came for a chat, Caleb told them his news with great excitement. Carrie and Julie hugged and both whispered, "Thank you!" to each other, then laughed. Carrie felt grateful to know that Caleb had such caring people looking out for him, she guessed a word in the right ear was all it took to start the ball rolling.

The only people Carrie didn't see much of all evening were Jane and Don. She saw them separately a couple of times, in the early evening and together, briefly, in the distance, a bit later. Everyone else had spent time talking to Caleb and herself except them. She hoped they hadn't fallen out or something. She was just wondering if she should text one of them when Caleb's parents arrived for a chat. She put on her best daughter in law smile and got ready to play her part. They were very nice people but hard work. Carrie wondered how Caleb was so broad-minded, when they were so set in their ways and, to be honest, a bit judgemental. Carrie was sure they still had no idea why Caleb had bought a farm or married her for that matter. He was probably supposed to marry some beautiful starlet, and live happily ever after in Hollywood, drowning in money or something. She was glad Caleb had the strength to be his own man.

At the end of the evening, or, more accurately, the early morning, as people went home, or searched out a bit of floor to sleep on, Carrie and Caleb headed up the track to Winnie, and to bed. Carrie was so pleased with the day, it had been even better than she expected. She felt so at peace with the world, and so in love with her husband. She was looking forward to getting back to normal now though. They still had their wedding night to look forward too, and their day of solitude on the cliffs tomorrow. After that, she would be glad to get back to rescuing animals with her friends, and her husband.

She hoped Caleb was happy with consummating their marriage softly and gently, after such a long day, she was feeling pretty stiff and sore. As they reached Winnie, they both stopped and laughed. Sometime during the day, someone had given Winnie a new look. She was covered in flowers and good luck wishes. Tied to the rear bumper were loads of old tin cans. Over the door, a huge, tacky sign read Newly Weds, and underneath was scrawled, 'Don't come knockin' if the van is rockin'. "We have such classy friends." grinned Caleb, as he opened the door. He turned to Carrie and lifted her into his arms. "I believe I should carry you over the threshold, my dear." He mounted the steps of the van and struggled to get them both through the door without hurting her. By the time they were inside they were both giggling so much, he nearly dropped her. He rushed over to the bed and lay her down safely.

"Oh Carrie, I am so tired but so happy, can we make love slowly and gently and then sleep for hours and hours?"

"Oh my love, that sounds perfect, apart from one thing."

"Anything, my love, just ask."

She giggled, "Can we have a cup of tea first, I'm gasping!?"

Chapter 25

Beginning

Carrie lay on the grass at the cliff edge, with Caleb asleep beside her. They had woken at 10am after a good lie in, had breakfast, then decided sunbathing was as much as they wanted to do all day.

The wedding night had progressed, pretty quickly, from drinking tea, to wonderful slow and sensual lovemaking. Carrie remembered every detail as she lay in the sun. Caleb had gently massaged her sore shoulders and neck for ages, his wonderful hands working out the knots of tension. Slowly her hands joined in, massaging him all over and enjoying the feel of his skin. When the massage had turned from love to lust, she couldn't remember, but they came together, stroking and feeling every inch of each other's bodies, with hands, tongues and lips. The feeling of love and passion, as they just explored each other, was overwhelming. When they finally came together, in the most intimate way, the feelings were amazing. She had never wanted it to end. She shattered under Caleb's hands and body so many times, she thought she might not survive. He drove her over the edge, time and again, his deep, passion filled voice urging her on. Finally, he reached his own shattering peak, taking her with him over the edge one more time. They stilled, breathing hard and totally spent.

She looked across at Caleb now, lying, sleeping beside her on the grass, in just a pair of well-cut trunks. She knew, very soon, she would wake him up with kisses and ask for a replay of last night's passion.

For now, she was happy to lie there, taking stock of their life. She'd been so unhappy a few days ago, she still didn't know why, maybe it was just wedding nerves, stirring up old feelings. She knew those sad feelings were gone for good now. She had no doubts, either about Caleb, or herself. This was where she was meant to be, he was who she was meant to be with. Their friends and family had shown them how happy they were for them, all was well. Life here would be hard work, and sad at times, but it was what they were meant to do.

Suddenly she thought of Don and Jane again and a cloud passed over her happiness. Don had asked her for help, before her accident, and she'd let him down, not been there for him. She picked up her phone and dialled his number. When he picked up, she went off into a long apologetic speech about letting him down, and that she was here for him now if he wanted to talk.

"Carrie, Carrie, breathe, I'm fine, we're fine. It's your honeymoon for God's sake, why are you worrying about me?"

"You rang me and asked to chat, and I let you down. I didn't see you at the wedding much, and I didn't see you with Jane, and I'm sorry if things aren't OK."

"Carrie, stop," Don was laughing now, "I'm fine, I'm in bed still. Don't worry, Josh is at the farm with Lynne, they are doing the animals. All is well."

"What about Jane, are you and she OK?"

"Carrie, you can ask her yourself, she's here, in bed, beside me, I can't make it any clearer without embarrassing myself but, WE ARE FINE, very fine in fact. We were just proving how FINE we are when you called. I'd kind of like to get back to that, if you're OK?"

Suddenly Carrie was laughing, "OH! You're FINE, I get it, sorry, I'm going, right now, I'm so happy for you both, enjoy! Does that sound weird? Sorry, love to Jane, I'm gone. Bye."

She could hear both Don and Jane laughing loudly as she hung up, Don must have put the phone on speaker. Carrie's cheeks burnt as she put the phone away, but that didn't stop the grin from breaking through. They were together, they were FINE for Pete's sake, what a perfect wedding gift to know they were properly together at last. She smiled at Caleb's sleeping form beside her.

"Time for us to feel FINE again my love," she said, gently, but urgently, kissing him awake.

THE END

for now.................

From the Author, Andrea Warrilow

Thank you so much for reading my book, I hope you enjoyed it, I loved writing it.

I have plans for at least two more books in this series so you don't need to say goodbye to Carrie, Caleb and friends yet.

In case you missed it, the first book in the series 'Cleaning the Slate' is still available as both an e-book (£2.99) and paperback (£7.99) on Amazon, or as a signed paperback direct from me at £7.99 plus £2.00 postage.

Please message me on my Facebook page 'Warrilow Writes', or under the same name on Twitter, if you would like a signed copy of any of my books. You can catch up on my latest news there too. If you don't do social media you can email me at 'flotsam@wimanx.net'.

Small spoiler alert, the next book will take a slightly darker and more mysterious twist. Let's just say Carrie gets in over her head when she turns detective. There will be plenty of animal and human relationships too. I'll say no more for now, mainly because most of it is still in my head and not yet written! It's going to be called 'Turning the Tide'.

If you bought this book online, please leave a review on Amazon – this really helps with future sales. If not, a comment or review on my Facebook or Twitter feeds is always welcomed. I enjoy constructive criticism too so feel free to be frank! I am still a writing novice and love to learn.

Thanks for reading.

Andrea xxx

About the Author

Andrea Warrilow is 54 and lives in the beautiful Isle of Man. She lives with her husband and mother along with her 2 dogs and 2 horses. It's crowded!!

She currently spends her time split between writing, working in the local village stores and caring for her mother who has reached a ripe old age. Obviously, any spare time is spent riding her horses or walking her dogs.

Everything else stops on a Tuesday when she spends the day volunteering for the Isle of Man group of Riding for the Disabled. Andrea started with RDA twelve years ago and has no plans to stop – ever! She is currently a group coach as well as a trustee and committee member. If you ever have free time please consider volunteering for your local RDA group. It is such a rewarding experience and great fun.

Printed in Poland
by Amazon Fulfillment
Poland Sp. z o.o., Wrocław